Threats

The Steamship Chronicles

Book Two

Margaret McGaffey Fisk

TTO
PUBLISHING

Cover art and design by Margaret McGaffey Fisk

Cover Photography and Text Graphics: Colin Fisk (photography) and Graechan (text graphics)

TTO Publishing logo design by Blue Harvest Creative
www.blueharvestcreative.com

Threats

Copyright 2014 by Margaret McGaffey Fisk

Published by
TTO Publishing

ISBN-10: 1-63139-009-0
ISBN-13: 978-1-63139-009-8

First Print Edition

Visit the author at:
Website: margaretmcgaffeyfisk.com
Twitter: @Marfisk
Google Plus: +MargaretMcGaffeyFiskAuthor
Facebook: MargaretMcGaffeyFisk

Other Works by
Margaret McGaffey Fisk

SEEDS AMONG THE STARS

(SCIENCE FICTION ADVENTURE)

Shafter

Trainee

The Captain's Chair (short story)

UNCOMMON LORDS AND LADIES

(SWEET REGENCY ROMANCES)

Beneath the Mask

A Country Masquerade

An Innocent Secret

THE STEAMSHIP CHRONICLES

(STEAMPUNK ADVENTURE)

Safe Haven (Prequel)

Threats

Gifts

Box Set 1 (Books 1-3)

SHORT STORIES (eBook only)

Forged

War Child

Curve of Her Claw (illustrated by Star Olsen)

*Visit margaretmcgaffeyfisk.com for more information
about these and other titles.*

1

S amantha?" Nat's whisper sounded overly loud with the engine shut down, but he didn't know how much time he had before Mister Garth returned from relieving himself over the side. A few days before, the engineer would never have considered letting Nat stay down there alone for even so short a time, and that was a trust he didn't want to lose. "Samantha?"

An icy chill raced down his spine when she didn't answer his repeated call.

The biscuit he'd saved from breakfast seemed little enough to sustain a body. He'd tried his best to save some-thing from every meal, but he hadn't managed each time. Nor had it always been possible to give what he'd reserved to her without arousing the engineer's suspicions.

Nat glanced toward the hatch, closed against the inclement weather, and slid between the copper pipes. He could always claim to have heard the hiss of steam escaping. Mister Garth had him wrap a weakened section just yesterday, the pipes old and worn as much as the rest of their vessel.

But she had a good heart and a good crew. He wouldn't choose to be on any other ship in the Company's fleet.

"Have you food?"

Nat slammed his head into a pipe, his reaction threatening to cause the very damage he'd hoped to use for an excuse. His teeth closed down over his tongue to hold back words his mother would have whipped him for speaking in the presence of a lady, no matter how threadbare and dirty her clothes.

"Not much for you, but it's what I was able to secret away."

How she managed to traverse the pipes with little more than a whisper of cloth he had no idea. She made him feel twice his size and more in the fashion of a bumbling circus bear than a man full grown.

She rubbed the back of one hand over her eyes, offering a hint as to her delayed response. "I have no right to complain. You've done so much for me, more than most others would have."

A wide grin spread across his face, and he ducked to hide the reaction to her praise. "It was nothing. No more than any decent fellow might do."

Out of the corner of his eye, he saw her shake her head, a movement that sent her lank hair to swaying, offering a hint of its beauty when properly tended. Sure, she had coal dust smeared across one cheek and grease under chipped nails, but Nat could sense she'd clean up right fine. Too fine for the likes of him no matter what his family had been, at least until he earned command of his own steamship.

"Can I have it?"

The hint of laughter in her voice made a wave of heat rush up from under his collar. Grateful for the dimly lit space, he dug out the biscuit. At the same time, he marveled over her change in demeanor now that she had food, irregular as her meals might be. He would never have mistaken her for a street child now.

Samantha took the biscuit from his hand and nibbled it slowly, requiring no reminder to make it last unlike the first time he'd offered her food in amongst the pipes. She no longer seemed feral, though he could not imagine any of the young ladies who'd made his acquaintance in his mother's drawing room managing these circumstances half so fair.

He lingered though he knew he should get back to the task of cleaning coal dust and soot from the valves, in this, a rare break from running the engine. Mister Garth had been almost as reluctant as the captain to shut it down, not wanting to end such a long run without trouble. Still, if the pipes clogged or the gears bound, they'd be back to where they'd been before, or maybe worse if the engine shook itself apart.

Nat twisted in the tight space, knowing his duty for all that Samantha fascinated him.

She stopped eating and brushed her fingers along his arm, enough to get his attention without restraining him.

Another young girl might have begged him to stay, desperate for the company, but Samantha had not shown that kind of weakness. If the isolation pained her, she would never sink him with the knowledge.

"I must be getting back. Mister Garth could return any moment."

"I don't mean to keep you," she said, her voice softer even than a whisper. "It's just I'd thought the trip to the Continent a short one. When will we make land?"

Nat sank to his heels, his body twined around the pipes in an uncomfortable fashion as he twisted back to look at her. His tongue felt heavy as his mind raced forward. He'd forgotten his decision not to burden her with where they were truly headed when he first learned of her existence. She couldn't have changed anything. By now, though, he'd thought she'd have figured it out.

"You still think we're bound to the Continent."

Her shoulders rose. "Where else?"

Between one heartbeat and the next, she went from self-sufficient and amazingly strong to a sheltered girl with no understanding of the ways of trade or sea passage.

A sigh rustled past Nat's lips. "If we'd been heading for the Continent, we wouldn't have been more than a day or so before the first port. Even those steaming up the Med stop in France or Spain to offload the post and the occasional passenger. It'll be a long time before you fetch up on those shores."

The darkness that shadowed her blue eyes told him her question had not been as much out of ignorance as he'd thought. He wished more than anything to wash her fears away. "Have you no one in the colonies?"

She shook her head, her jaw tightening in the way he'd grown used to seeing when she set her mind to something even with their short acquaintance. "None I know of." She sucked in a breath. "I'll manage. I've gotten this far."

Her reaction startled a laugh out of him. "You'll go much farther before we're done. Don't worry. Captain Paderwatch has a good head for the trades, and he gives us each a share of the earnings once his costs are repaid. I should net enough to buy you passage back home, or on to the Continent, once we reach land."

"You've done so much."

He didn't have the chance to reply because the steady clomp of boot heels approaching thudded overhead, an affectation the engineer maintained even when anyone beyond the officers went barefoot.

After a quick wave goodbye, he turned and started winding through the pipes to get into place, leaving Samantha to her limited repast and even slimmer hopes.

He should have told her, if not when she'd first revealed the misunderstanding, then any number of times since. How had he failed to consider the impact of each day passing as her belief in their destination slowly crumbled? Her strength might have been born of the understanding that her ordeal would soon end, something she could no longer hold on to.

Their passage would be measured in weeks. The runs across the Channel took a fraction of that time.

He'd survive on short rations, but she'd suffer more than he would, especially with little hope of giving her anything other than stew-soaked bread. Even without the difficulty of the dishes, he had no way to hold back his porridge or stew without raising the very suspicions they both needed to avoid.

Nat slipped back amongst the soot-darkened valves and picked up his rag just in time.

The hatch swung open, and Mister Garth stomped his way down to the chamber.

Though he bent to his task, Nat's thoughts spun a familiar revolution. He questioned, as he had many times before, the wisdom of giving in to her pleas not to tell the captain back when they'd been no more than a few days out. The consequences to their schedule if they'd turned back then were not to be considered, but how could he have let her become the very rats he'd suspected her of being, living in hiding with only crumbs to sustain her.

Despite her fears, the captain was a good man.

Nat sighed. Whatever he thought now, he could not reveal her without making his involvement obvious.

"Don't be so glum, Mister Bowden. It might be dirty work, but it's important. Think back on when you woulda done anything to get permission to come through that hatch. You got what you'd wished for."

Mister Garth gave a laugh that held a gruff edge but none of the bitterness Nat had first faced from the engineer. He'd gone a long way toward proving his worth to the man, and nothing would convince him to give up the gains.

Not that he'd been frowning over the task, anyway. If the engineer thought it grimier than scrubbing down the deck boards, he'd been too long below.

Nat let the teasing pass without comment, more so he wouldn't be pushed to explain the true source of his upset than out of any need to suffer it.

The way Samantha's predicament gnawed at his mind, he'd be hard pressed not to fail both her and himself in blurting out his concerns. He had no right to share them with anyone, certainly not the self-same man who, a short time ago, was willing to see Nat hang on the suspicion of theft. How much more harshly would Garth deal with one who'd stowed away?

2

S am stared after Nat for a long while, the biscuit hanging forgotten in her limp fingers. Her mind churned with suspicions turned to fact as though the bent gears she'd replaced in the ship engine infested her thoughts.

In the confusion of the docks and under the influence of the steam engine's cry, she'd never considered the many destinations a ship could seek. She'd had little time to ruminate on such thoughts between fighting the aether-laced demands and just as powerful hunger pangs, but even so she'd started to wonder at how slow they'd taken what Henry believed an easy passage.

Now Nat's sacrifice seemed so much greater.

When she'd begged him to keep her secret, it had seemed a simple request. He had known just how long she'd been asking for even if she had not. And he planned to do more when he must have a family counting on whatever returns he could manage.

She clenched her fists, stopping only when she realized her motion would crush the biscuit and scatter its crumbs. As little as the dry bread offered, she needed every bit of it and she refused to waste what Nat gave up.

Another person who risked everything for her just as her sister Lily had done when not much older than Sam was now. No matter how much she tried, her gift got in the way, and got others in trouble.

The steam engine whispered in the back of her mind, aether-driven promises reminding her of one bout that had aided rather than harmed—the engine repairs. Only now the engine wanted more, more power, smoother running, and the chance to be so much better than it had ever been.

Sam shoved the biscuit into her mouth, almost choking on the dry, floury taste of it. She focused on the process of chewing, trying to savor each bite and stave off the vulnerability that would let the engine in.

Her one success, her one time where she did what she needed to fix the engine instead of transforming it into something the others could not handle, and it threatened to trick her into doing more. The engine cried out for changes like those she did to the steam carriage, changes which had cost her a carefully scheduled trip to the Continent with enough money in her purse and a hire carriage to take her where she needed to go.

A laugh escaped her at the memory before she remembered to make no noise.

At least Nat had been talking at the same moment, and it seemed neither of the sailors noticed her slip.

She would not have to take her friend's slender earnings after all. She had the means to buy her own passage back in the pouch Henry had given her, or at least enough to pay part.

The coins had been tucked into her boots for so long she'd forgotten they existed. Sam had no need for money when pressed to the ship wall. It couldn't fill her stomach or help her hide from sailors who'd be quick enough to punish her for her presence.

Sam pulled the pouch free and shoved it into her pocket. She had coin enough to pay for her passage. She'd give it to

Nat to buy her place once they found port. Out here in the vast ocean, though, they would not be able to use her money to buy the extra supplies needed to take on a passenger.

Elation rushed through her where she'd expected despair, carrying with it a tingle Sam almost didn't recognize in time. The engine had found a crack in her resistance.

She fought the urge to wrap herself in aether and forget all her troubles while she made the engine's dreams into reality. Only memory of the steam carriage, of the coachman's shouts that soon became screams as the carriage leapt out of his control, kept her from jumping from her hiding spot. She wanted to brush past both Nat and the engineer to reorder the engine's gears into a better pattern so it could race this old boat across the waves, turning a long voyage into half the time as long as it could hold together under the pressure.

Sam released her grip on the pipe standing between her and the open space where she'd be exposed, only then aware she'd gone.

She owed Nat for what he'd done for her, and what he planned to do. Her actions had cost him too much pain already. Sam would not add to it evidence both of her presence and that Nat had been feeding her from the precious stores, for who else came down into the engine room besides Mister Garth? No one would believe Nat shorted his own portions from what she'd seen.

No matter how much the engine wound its way into her thoughts and desires, she refused to repay Nat's kindness with more of the disasters that followed in her wake ever since she'd left Henry's property for the world beyond it.

First Lily, then Henry, and now Nat had been strong for her.

This time Sam would be strong on her own, strong enough to avoid both bringing more trouble down on Nat's head and tearing this old ship apart by giving in to the steam engine's dreams of power.

Mister Garth worked one side of the engine and Nat the other as they cleared the fire's soot before it caused clogs that would damage the machinery. When they met at the middle, Mister Garth caught sight of Nat and laughed. "You'll fit right in at the docks in the colonies, boy. Many a black face there. You and Hassan both."

Nat didn't feel comfortable enough with the engineer's teasing to return the comment as he looked at Mister Garth's darkened features. No way could they avoid the painting when they had to lean in close to get every last bit of dust off the precious engine.

His tongue might have been reserved, but Nat's stomach had no reluctance when it came to making its feelings known.

"That how it is then? Having a boy down here means a meal clock steadier even than the ship's bells. I'll just check on some final adjustments and make sure you didn't knock anything awry with your efforts. You run ahead. Warn Jenson to serve us right up. And draw a bucket of seawater to wash. The food won't taste any better with coal grit lining your tongue."

Nat didn't hesitate, his stomach fighting the short rations, especially after a long morning scrubbing the engine.

He lifted the hatch and blinked at the light beyond, understanding the owlish look on Mister Garth's face better now that he spent his time in the dim of the engine room.

"Turning into a chimney sweep, Mister Bowden? Or just jealous." Hassan flipped upside down from where he had been working the rigging, his teeth bright against his dark skin.

Nat waved at the sailor. "I couldn't hope to match your chocolate. I'm off to the scrub bucket." Of all the crew, those aloft had been the ones to stand by him in his earlier troubles. He missed his time among them, vying for the first sight of land and who was fastest up to the tall mast. Mister Garth kept him too busy, though, and he had other responsibilities he could not shirk. Still, from their cheerful greetings whenever he came onto deck or they passed in the below quarters, the sail teams did not hold it against him.

Nat ducked below to the sound of Hassan's rich laughter. He had first to warn Jenson Garth would be coming for his meal soon.

The cook offered up more teasing about his state when he passed the message as did each of the sailors he crossed paths with. They reminded him how working with them had been a cleaner, fresher, or otherwise more attractive job.

Despite the words, he heard a touch of envy in their tones.

Not a one among them hadn't shared with him the desire to know more about their engine a time or two since he'd come aboard. Yet only he had won the privilege, though the process almost cost his life.

He let them carry on with their teasing. It was little enough to endure considering he'd been allowed into the one place held more sacred than even the captain's quarters.

By the time Nat reached the scrub bucket, he had a grin plastered on his face and a nod already prepared for the next greeting. His mother would have fainted at the sight of him, dirtier even than the time he'd thought to help the farmhands and slipped in the pig pen.

Here, though, he had no fancy soaps and washcloths, nor did he need to pass under the close eye of their housekeeper.

Nat threw the bucket over the side and raised it full of salt water rough enough to scrape away the worst grime. His shirt offered cloth, and he no longer hesitated to strip down in front of the other sailors. He scrubbed and scrubbed until his skin stung and the water in the bucket held too much of the black to lighten the gray of his shirt when he rinsed the fabric.

Nat pulled the shirt back over his head, not willing to chance it going overboard, and tossed the bucket full of black into the arms of the ocean. He jerked the bucket at the end of the line several times before pulling it back up once again filled with clean, if brackish, water.

"The bucketful for me, Mister Bowden?" the engineer asked, choosing that moment to join Nat at the rail.

"I thought you might want a wash as well."

Mister Garth lowered his eyebrows in a scowl that once had the ability to scare Nat. "You saying I'm not clean enough for your liking?"

Nat could hear the humor in the engineer's gruff tone, something lacking before the captain forced them into each other's company. This time he knew just what to say. "An engineer once told me it was a waste of food to eat after cleaning the engine unless you washed first."

"A wise man that was indeed, Mister Bowden, and advice I'm happy to follow. You go collect our meals and meet me up by the bow. The rush of fresh air cleans where not even the most diligent of scrubs can reach, though you'll be blowing soot out of your nose for many days to come, you mark my words."

Nat pulled himself together and wiped the shock from his expression, grateful the engineer had bent to his cleaning while speaking his offhanded invitation to sup alongside him. The man had laid claim to the bow long before Nat arrived on this vessel, and not even Mister Trupt, their first mate, saw fit to join him there.

"Well, get on with you, boy. Our supper's getting none the warmer for the delay. If your belly's half as empty as mine it won't thank you for the lagging."

A flush heated the back of Nat's neck as he scrambled to follow the engineer's command. He should have been able to accept the invitation graciously instead of gaping like a fool, but he'd do his best to be a good companion and make up for his indiscreet surprise.

Nat headed for the bow, two bowls clutched in his arms and the bread already soaking up the rich stew. His passage caught the notice of more than one crewman, especially when he returned their greetings with a nod and a smile but did not stop.

The crew split into groups often by function, friendships grown strong over shared labors. He'd worked with all of them in his attempt to understand the least workings of the ship, whether scrubbing the deck or swaying far above it. He'd gone among them in leisure as well, listening to their tales and soaking up the wisdom of the sea.

This meal, though, he wove his way past each and every one of them, not even pausing to exchange a word or two. Mister Garth's invitation spoke of more than just spooning stew, and Nat didn't want to start out by offering a meal gone cold because he lingered.

"Let me take one of those off your hands," Mister Garth said as Nat neared the bow.

He gratefully relinquished the engineer's share, his arm seared by the hot clay even through his still-damp shirt.

"Come, Mister Bowden. Sit right up here and breathe deep. It'll clear the last of the soot from your lungs, it will."

Nat followed the directions only to cough fiercely as the damp air scoured his lungs clear.

Mister Garth snatched the second bowl from Nat's loosened grip and pounded him hard on the back with his free hand. "Now no need to go wasting a good stew."

When his lungs had cleared, Nat accepted his stew back, still unable to overcome his amazement at spending time with the grouchy engineer by choice, and even more at the respect in the engineer's eyes as Mister Garth tapped the spot at his side.

"We had a rough beginning, Mister Bowden, but I've seen how you work with the rest of the crew. Hard not to notice with you running back and forth, always doing something for someone when you're not keeping the captain entertained. Used to bother me to tell the truth. Thought you were nothing but trouble, always underfoot, getting in everyone's business."

Nat opened his mouth to protest, but the engineer put a hand out to stop him.

"Now don't be getting your dander up. I said used to. The captain forcing you on me seemed a punishment undeserved, but I've come to see you're a handy, willing boy. You haven't an underhanded bone in your body. Not one to go spreading tales or withholding truths you are. Nor do you expect the crew to wait on you, though I'd guess you have a full staff where you call home, am I right?"

A stiff nod was all Nat could offer, hoping the engineer would credit his flush to embarrassment at the praise.

"You're a good boy, and polite to boot. Don't you let my rumbles keep you from your food. Dig in. We need all the energy we can get what with maintaining the engine. She's never run steady this long before, and I aim to keep her smooth as a baby's bum. Just 'cause she's old doesn't mean she has no value. Mark my words. If we make a fine haul on our goods, it'll be half planning and half steam that it will."

Nat grunted in agreement even as he thrust two fingers into the stew, cooling but still warm enough to heat his skin. With his mouth full, he'd be better able to hold his tongue in the face of Mister Garth's good mood. To gain the engineer's respect had seemed an impossible task such a short time ago, and now that he had, he didn't deserve the praise. For his work, sure, but not for his manner, not with lies of omission weighing heavy on him.

Mister Garth proved a man slow to trust, but firm in his belief once he'd warmed to a body. How much more valuable his praise when it came hard won, and how much harder it would be to see that respect vanish if Nat's deceit became known. Yet, it wasn't his secret to keep, or his to tell. He'd promised Samantha.

Sea voyages had little of the consistency found on land, and resources took space from trade goods. They were measured within a few pounds of their needs. Nat had no experience in the treatment of stowaways, but he'd heard enough tales to know the judgment to be swift and the punishment harsh. He could not chance the crew's reaction to her discovery, not even if it meant his conscious burned him.

Samantha had done nothing but attempt to carry out her guardian's wishes.

Through no fault of her own, the plans laid for her had fallen to pieces. He would not be the cause of her failure. If he'd come to enjoy her company in the few stolen moments they managed, it was little enough recompense for sharing his portions.

The reminder stilled his hand when he'd all but scraped the bowl clean.

He glanced over to find Mister Garth bent to the task of filling his stomach as well, most likely unused to company as he'd eaten alone in the whole time Nat had known him.

Taking advantage of the engineer's preoccupation, Nat scooped his bread along the bowl's curve, collecting what he could then tucked the stew-soaked loaf into a linen handkerchief his mother had sent along with him, now well stained.

She'd never have imagined either the mockery he would suffer if he used this to wipe his brow, or the use he found for it now. Deep down inside, he thought his mother would approve of his purpose. He'd been taught from an early age to respect the females in his life, a harsh lesson when his little sister took it upon herself to trail after him wherever he'd tried to go, but one he'd learned well. She would never have countenanced him turning Samantha over to the rough justice of the crew.

That thought did little to comfort his still aching belly, but it would have to be enough to keep his head held high around Mister Garth and the others. Nat had learned the value of appearances well enough after being accused of theft. When he'd protested his innocence at every turn, even the crew who'd supported him began to question their loyalty. The realization served him well once he had a real lie to conceal after discovering the true thief to be Samantha scavenging desperately for the food she needed to survive.

"All right then, Mister Bowden. You ready to give the pipes a thorough checking? I must say I appreciate a younger, limber body ready to investigate those in the back. Squeezing through ain't the most comfortable for a man of my stature."

Nat's chest tightened not at the thought of Mister Garth squeezing into the back spaces between the pipes, but at what he'd find if he traced the metal tubes all the way to the ship's wall.

"I'm happy to do it," Nat said, the words coming out in a rush and causing the engineer to raise an eyebrow.

"Mighty eager, you are. Let's see how the day treats you once we're done. It's a tiring chore, but one which can save the ship and all those within it should we need to steam our way through a storm or two as is common on this run. Best get to it, and quickly, before you rethink the glamor of twisting through spaces designed for someone a might bit smaller even than you."

The engineer clapped Nat on the back as they both rose.

Nat collected the bowls for Jenson and ran ahead to drop them with the cook. He arrived at the hatch only moments after Mister Garth, determined the engineer would not put it into his head to check the joints himself after all. Even if Samantha could find a spot distant enough to hide, the slight signs of her habitation would stand out where there should be no sign of food or fingerprints at all.

5

S am had little to do in her tight space, especially since returning the gears. She leaned against the rough wood wall and listened to the vibrations of the engine. The hum of chatter among the sailors and occasional footsteps offered an odd counterpoint, but not enough to amuse.

Her hemline showed signs of fraying. She'd picked at the caked dirt so often the fabric gave way, but she no other form of amusement.

Her fingers itched for something to do.

Limited nutrition offered the only barrier between her and an aether-driven bout.

She had enough sustenance to keep her going, but none to spare.

Much of the time, Sam drifted in and out of sleep, dreaming the steam engine's dreams when her own proved less powerful. Nat's visits were her only high point in this endless voyage.

As though conjured by her thoughts, the hatch opened and Nat's light footsteps came down the stairs.

Sam jerked free of the engine's hold and slid between the pipes toward the entrance. Nat only returned so quickly after a meal when he had something for her. He thought she waited on whatever portion he could save from his own plate. In truth, she treasured his company.

The starvation hardly bothered her with such a limited space to move in. Besides, keeping her energy low enough to ignore the engine's pleas could mean the difference between arriving safely on dry land once again, even if that land stretched an ocean distant from where she wanted to be, and sinking into the water she could feel and hear rushing against the hull.

Her shoulder slammed into a pipe, Sam gone clumsy in her eagerness, but Nat was the one to let loose a sailor's curse.

"Be careful in there," the engineer said, sending Sam back three steps before another pipe caught at her heels. "It's a small space, but better I squeeze into it than you damage more than you can repair."

"I guess I was a little too eager to see past the pipes. I'll take care."

The engineer laughed at Nat's statement, though it made Sam smile.

"There's nothing past the first row of pipes other than more pipes. Hope you're not still hunting those invisible rats."

"I won't know until I see with my own eyes."

"Young men and their dreams."

The engineer sighed, but Sam no longer cared as Nat had reached her and held a finger to his lips.

"You at the hull yet? Start at the back and work your way forward. Check the joints just like I showed you, but run a hand along the pipes too. They're old and this is a lot of strain. Maybe I should have you sweet talk the pipe makers next."

Nat twisted back to stare toward the engineer as though startled.

Sam brushed a hand against his knee in question, but he only shook his head.

"I'm happy to help," he called after a moment.

"That you are. And maybe there's a use for your eagerness after all. The parts sure kept us running smooth."

A broad grin took over Nat's face, one so full of joy she felt her own lips curve in turn.

The engineer continued on, unaware of a conversation he could not hear. "They're a prideful bunch, as if sitting around in a workshop is better work than out on the waters. Like to talk down to a sailing engineer, but a wide-eyed boy? That must have been a treat for them. No wonder they bent over backwards and handed over the highest quality. Wanted to show off. Your baby-faced innocence won't last long out here. We should make use of it while we can."

Nat whispered under this, the longest speech she'd heard from the engineer. "I have food for you from supper, but I'm here to check the pipes."

Sam nodded in acknowledgment and accepted a bundle in finer linen than she'd seen outside of Henry's manor. It explained a lot if Nat came from a family like Lily's husband had. A true-born sailor might have been less welcoming of her presence.

She tucked the bundle into her skirt pocket along with Henry's purse, and slid between the pipes, heading not for her corner but to the first of the weaknesses the engine had shown her.

Nat didn't follow, so she turned back and waved him on.

His brow creased in a frown, but she kept gesturing until he shrugged and came, probably worried she'd call out next. After all, he had no idea she could sense the engine, but this way she could help both the mechanical that still haunted her dreams and the ship carrying her onward to land.

Nat gave her a grin when he came to understand her purpose. He raised a piece of coal she hadn't noticed in his other hand and marked one stroke. "Found one," he called to the engineer.

"Needs tying off?"

Nat shook his head then ducked it as a flush colored his cheeks. "No, just watching," he said to the engineer, having first responded silently more used to talking that way with her.

Sam moved on.

This time Nat didn't hesitate. He reached the next spot she'd noticed right at her side. A whistle came from between his teeth. "Found another, and this one—well, it's a miracle it didn't break apart already."

"Mark it with two strokes, but if it's that bad, you come right back now and get the ties. Can't have her falling apart on us."

Sam had noticed in listening to Mister Garth how he referred to the engine as a person at times, even stroking the mechanical sides. What he lacked in skill, he made up for in care, and Sam felt a bond between them despite the engineer being unaware of her presence.

Nat made his two marks as she braced the pipe with both hands.

The heat seared her palms, steam still venting from the boiler even with the engine down, but it would do no good for even soft strokes with the charcoal to push the pieces apart and send steam gushing over both of them.

She buried the reddened skin in her skirt and waited for Nat to head back to the engineer.

As soon as he left, she sought one of the pipes that carried cold salt water in for the engine's use. Sam held in a sigh of relief at the chill touch, her heated palms slowly leaching the burn out until the wall of pipe held a measure of warmth and her skin no longer burned.

Mister Garth must have been showing Nat how to tie off the weakened joint because her friend had yet to return. With the pain in her hands diminished, Sam's curiosity led her to creep closer to the front where she could hear the directions. Aether might tell her how the parts came together, but the engineer had years of experience in repairing the engine, years no instinct could replace, especially without the parts on hand to draw the aether.

6

A nd make sure you tie the knot double. Does no good to work on the pipes then do it so it can't hold against the jolting of the waves. You've done well enough out here, but don't get all sloppy where I can't see you."

Nat tightened his fingers around the strips of canvas, sliced from sail too far gone to repair. "I won't." He choked on an instinctive "I swear," remembering the first mate's advice not to be too free with his swears.

From the sharp look Mister Garth sent his way, though, the thought had been heard even unspoken.

"Those ain't the words you need to be watching, Mister Bowden. You've been aboard long enough to know better."

Nat shook his head in confusion as he raced his mind through everything he'd said, mostly "Yes" and "I understand," since climbing free of the pipes.

"You're so quick sometimes I forget how young you are, and how little time you've spent as a sailor even since you climbed the ramp. Miracles, boy. That's the word not to use. Don't be calling God's eye down like you did just now in the pipes, or hinting that something's come to watch over us. Good or bad, more trouble will brew when such words are dangled in front of the sailors. Superstitious lot they are."

"Sorry." He'd forgotten what he'd called out while with Samantha until this reminder. Nat turned toward the pipes with a shrug, accepting the advice but not sure it had been worth the telling.

He stopped suddenly as Mister Garth's hand closed on one shoulder hard enough to pinch.

The engineer waited until Nat twisted round to continue, "This is no idle talk, Mister Bowden. No, it surely ain't. You go telling them we have a miracle brewing in the engine room, and they'll be sneaking down to touch the joint for luck. They'll knock who knows how many out in the process, and call the luck bad when the engine fails." Mister Garth grimaced. "A sailor's life is at the mercy of the elements. No amount of skill can carry you through a voyage without luck on your side. A sailor will do anything to make sure of enough good luck, no matter what the barriers."

Nat laughed. "You don't know your own strength of personality, Mister Garth. Any one of the sailors would love a peek at what you hide down here, but not a one has ever—or will ever—test your good nature by coming through that door uninvited."

"You're a fool if you believe that, Bowden. You bandy about the miracle word and maybe they'll keep out from respect while things are going well. Respect for me? Unlikely. But luck, that they understand. Only have a storm blow too long, or the engine take us a bit off course, and your miracle turns on its head."

The engineer's eyes clouded over as though seeing into some horrible past or terrifying future. "You'll have sailors muttering under their breaths about the engine being cursed, about a witch brewing who knows what over the engine fire. It took a lot for the crew to come to terms with an engine in the first place, and worse, one that requires a constant flame below decks. Won't take much to turn them against her. Then see if fear of my scowl keeps them from taking an axe to that hatch and everything they can reach down here."

Any humor Nat had mustered when Mister Garth began drained away in the face of the last statement. "They wouldn't."

"They would. Never misjudge the strength of fear. It's a powerful force, and not something even a thinking man can counter."

"I—" Nat choked on the words, then swallowed and let them free. "I swear I'll keep my tongue between my teeth. I won't be the cause of any risk to the ship or the engine."

That won him a slight smile from Mister Garth. The engineer glanced toward the mass of metal gears and steam. "She's the heart of the ship, you know. There's many who won't say so, who think engines the worst of the changes wrought, but if the sails make up her wings, the steam engine pumps life through her wooden bones. If you remember that much, you'll do well."

The reverent look faded from the engineer's expression so suddenly it was as though a candle had been blown out. The more familiar scowl settled on Mister's Garth's features as he glowered at Nat. "But not for a long time, boy, you hear me? You have a lot to learn. It's not so easy to be an engineer. Takes years before you'll understand even a fraction of her workings."

Nat couldn't understand what brought the gruffness back to the engineer's tones, but he had no interest in arguing the point. Even had the engineer's position been his goal, he wouldn't want to take it too soon.

If the sailors could turn against the engine based on rumor alone, how much worse would it be to win a position he lacked the skill for and have all the crew dependent on abilities he hadn't taken the time to earn?

"I'd best get back to securing the pipes," he said, raising the hand holding canvas strips.

Mister Garth blinked, and the tension drained from his shoulders. "That you should. Those pipes won't hold if we hit a bad storm. Every piece is important, Mister Bowden. Every person has a role to play. You remember what I said."

"I will."

Nat didn't stay around for any more admonishments.

He couldn't tell whether Mister Garth meant the warning not to get a swelled head or the one against playing on sailors' superstitions, but both seemed worth keeping in mind. The first would secure him in the engineer's favor while the second...he'd seen the power of rumor first hand when Mister Garth thought he'd taken food not set aside for his own belly. He'd starve himself to share with Samantha before he'd ever consider chancing the penalties awaiting a crewman found claiming more than he deserved from the stores.

The engineer's good mood had not returned by the time Nat climbed out of the pipes as the dinner bell sounded, and no offer of a place up on the bow was made.

Nat chose to join the riggers when Jenson handed him a bowl of thick stew and a biscuit rather than seeking out Captain Paderwatch. The fare might have been better at the captain's table, but he preferred the sight of the stars above him, and the chance to crash in his hammock once he'd lined his belly instead of working navigation charts all night. Mister Garth had spoken faithfully about the exhaustion to follow their day's labors.

"Suppin' with your betters tonight?" one of the riggers said as Nat sank to the deck.

The sun's warmth still lingered in the boards, and it eased some of the tension gathered in his muscles. He'd twisted and squeezed his way through the pipes for hours, following the wisp that was Samantha. "Where else would I go for the best word on what's been happening across the ship?"

The man laughed, and the rest joined in. "Not much escapes our eyes, young Bowden, as you should know. A princely perspective it is from up on the ropes. Though I suppose you have news of your own what with spending all your time below deck. How goes our engine?"

Nat could see the curiosity reflected in many of the faces surrounding him, but Mister Garth's warning kept his words brief. "Dark."

That drew a second laugh from the gathering, and the focus moved from him to teasing one of the riggers who'd lost his grip earlier that day. As with when Nat had been learning, the teasing served both to ease the strain of what might have happened, and as a reminder not to make the same mistake again.

"I wouldn't have slipped at all if I hadn't spent half my rest learning fancy figures and ciphering. What need I to calculate my share anyhow? Not like the captain would cheat us, and if he did, we'd have to say, 'thank you, Captain, sir,' and accept whatever he handed our way. Most captains wouldn't give any, much less a fair measure," the man grumbled.

"A little figuring never did you any harm," Nat said without thinking, repeating what his tutor had handed him in return for his complaints.

"Easy enough for you to say," another of the men joined in. "The captain's new interest in teaching us our ciphering didn't start until you disappeared into the engine room."

Nat heard enough bitterness in the statement to know the teasing had gone too far. He raised his hands in surrender, half regretting the decision to avoid the captain a little while longer. "There's times when I wouldn't mind sitting in front of a navigation chart."

He attempted to launch into a funny rendition of his day spent sliding through pipes designed with a weasel in mind rather than any man or boy, but never even got started. The men he'd considered mates if not friends drowned out his efforts with their complaints.

"Hold on now. You know as well as I do Nat had none of the choosing in going down there. If he's made his peace with the arrangement, who are you to judge him? He's spending his days ducking heads to the same man as tried to stretch him

from the yardarm not so long ago." Phil made a gesture familiar to all of them, and Nat could almost feel the rough rope
that had come so close to closing about his neck. "Besides,
who are we to complain about a smidge of learning? Between
the work Mister Bowden has done, and those magical engine
parts he got from the shipyard, the whole trip will be safer and
shorter than it's been since they put the beast in our belly.
We'll be needing the skill of counting out our shares that
much sooner, and the coin piles will stand a might bit taller, all
thanks to this young man."

Phil clapped Nat on the shoulder, a big grin on the man's
face, but Nat fought back a shudder. He had only to see the
reverent looks that took over the expressions around him to
remember once again Mister Garth's warning, this time with a
better understanding of its weight.

A beast Phil had called the engine, but with the voyage so
far in their favor, a beast to be appreciated. If a little extra
schooling to keep the captain entertained caused this much
discontent, how much would come the moment the engine
slipped a gear and faltered, as it had many times since Nat had
climbed aboard.

He pushed to his feet, grateful for the hunger that had
cleaned his plate all unnoticed as the others bantered back and
forth. His dishes offered enough of an excuse, and he didn't
have to try hard to bring forth a yawn. "As long as we're running smooth, I'll get what rest I can. Who knows the tasks set
to me come morning."

Their good moods restored, the riggers sent him off to a
chorus of fair wishes, but Nat had seen enough to know his
association with the engine, with Phil's beast, had become
firmly fixed in their minds. It had wiped out all the times he'd
climbed the ropes with them, scrubbed the pans for Jenson, or

done a myriad of other tasks. And if the engine fell out of favor, how quickly would they turn on him?

Such thoughts did not make for a restful sleep, though exhaustion soon drew him into fitful dreams.

8

$\mathcal{M}$orning dawned without the bright sunlight they'd grown used to, and Nat stumbled up on deck to find preparations for a storm that threatened on the horizon already underway. Every sailor had a purpose in securing the ship. Loose sails could be torn to shreds, shore boats thrown about would become a hazard to any still above decks, and anything not secured could vanish beneath the rough waters.

Nat ducked around the deck workers and ran for the lines, his responsibility to help with securing the wind-tossed sail. Sailcloth was always the first to react to a coming storm and it required many hands to gather and tie down.

"Mister Bowden."

The first mate's voice managed to carry through the chaos of shouts, running feet, and lashing wind right to Nat's ears.

He stumbled, stopping so quickly his feet had no notion of where they belonged.

A rough hand steadied him, but before he could express his gratitude, the deck hand nudged him toward Mister Trupt. It wouldn't do to keep the first mate waiting, especially not in the midst of storm preparations.

"Yes, sir." Nat's breathless voice had little to do with the wind and more with his sprint to the stern.

"What do you think you're doing, Mister Bowden?" The first mate frowned down at him.

Nat curled his shoulders to ward off a blow he didn't understand. "I was heading aloft. You assigned me with the last two storms." He knew he shouldn't have added the last. One didn't argue with Mister Trupt, not when he wore that look.

The first mate took Nat by the shoulders and turned him bodily. "That was before, when climbing proved your strongest skill. You're needed below."

He gave a strong enough push that Nat started toward the engine hatchway before he had time to catch the first mate's meaning. Instead of a punishment set by the captain, it seemed he'd become the engineer's unofficial apprentice in the eyes of the crew. This, more even than Phil's defense the night before, made Nat's back straighten and a smile play at his lips despite the dangers crawling toward them across the waters.

The hatch slammed open, almost taking off his toes.

Mister Garth stuck his head up and looked around for a moment before catching sight of Nat. "There you are. What are you waiting for? That storm looks to be a bad one, and we have more work to do if we hope to steam our way through it."

"Yes, sir." Nat ducked his head to hide a grin as he followed the engineer down into the dark space below deck. He did not intend to take an engineer's path, but how better to understand such a critical working of a ship than to strive alongside the man who kept it running, especially through a storm. It wouldn't harm his reputation among the crew either should he be part of the force that drove them free of it instead of battening down the hatches and praying not to capsize.

9

The storm hit soon after Nat entered the engine room, darkening the space even further, and the water in the air made it seem tighter than usual. The oil lantern sputtered and swayed, turning an already busy space into a nightmare of places to slam into as the floor bucked and heaved.

"Keep the coal coming, Mister Bowden. We need this fire strong."

Nat headed over to the coal bin, tossed first into the stairs and then the pipes before he managed to grab the edge of the bin and pull himself against it.

Mister Garth made no comment, despite the chance of damage, a sure sign of the danger.

A hiss and clank warned of another pipe fixture come free, but Nat could not think about it. He had to fill his sack with coal and make his way back to the fire. On a normal day, he'd fill a shovel or two, feed the fire, and move on to other tasks. With the storm turning the engine room into a smoke-filled, dark, thick trap and the floor coming up to meet him one moment and dropping away in the next, a shovel offered no hope of success.

Mister Garth cursed, but the words cut off sharply as the engineer slid past Nat on a floor that had suddenly become a wall.

Nat thrust out an arm, keeping the other clamped to the edge of the bin.

The engineer caught hold, wrenching Nat's shoulder, but coming to a halt. He climbed hand over hand up Nat's arm until he too could grab the secured coal bin.

"Tell me you didn't let the coal bag fall," Mister Garth said as soon as they stood face to face.

Nat pointed to his waistband where he'd secured the bag with the intent of struggling back up to the fire. "I wasn't expecting to catch you, but I wasn't chancing a wasted trip if it came free from my hand."

Whatever the engineer would have said in response was lost as the ship sank down another trough, and they went sliding toward the engine.

Nat focused his efforts on landing soft enough to keep his bruises from getting any worse, and Mister Garth seemed to do the same. They came to a stop side by side, less than an arms-length from the heated wall of the potbelly iron stove that belched smoke and hissed from the water condensing on its heated surface.

"Take these strips and find that pipe," Mister Garth commanded. "I'll feed the fire. From the feel of these seas, our best hope lies in keeping the engine going long enough to drive us out the other side. The damage will be bad enough without sitting still while the water and rain pounds us."

10

Sam teased the frayed edge of her skirt until she freed another strip to tear.

The rocking threw her back against the hull, but with her feet braced, she didn't lose her position or drift away from the pipe she needed to secure.

She'd listened carefully to the engineer's explanation the previous day, never thinking she'd need it so quickly. All her restraint would mean nothing if the ship broke apart in the storm.

The ship bucked and the joint she'd been about to wrap separated, dousing her in brackish water. Sam choked and shook the wet hair out of her face, but didn't move away from the stream.

She'd been lucky. Instead of severe burns with no way to treat them, she'd gotten the closest thing to a wash she'd had since leaving home. But a steam engine couldn't work without steam, and if she didn't get this pipe back in line, the chamber would fill with water, and the engine would die.

Blinded by the gush of liquid, she struggled to place her strips of cloth, jerking back when her fingers encountered flesh instead of metal.

Nat stood on the other side, his gaze not on her, but on the separated pipes.

Sam blinked the salt from her eyes and grabbed the pipe to steady it for him.

He glanced at her for just a heartbeat, giving her a quick smile, before turning back to the task neither could manage alone.

His thick canvas strips made for a stronger bond, and soon the salt water raced toward the engine where it would be heated into steam instead of drowning both the fire and them.

"Thank you."

Sam read Nat's lips more than heard him over the clash of noises from the storm, the rumble of gears struggling to stay aligned, and the slosh of water now ankle deep in the chamber. She didn't even try for speech, nodding in acknowledgment before reaching out to the aether to find the next weak point.

The engine screamed along the connection like a dying calf.

Sam collapsed onto the waterlogged floor, her nerves screaming along with the engine.

She'd never suffered from aether's call before, but then neither had she reached out to a mechanical in distress.

"Are you all right?"

The words, shouted into her ear, made Sam aware Nat bent over her, worry wrinkling his forehead.

She swallowed hard and choked at the salt still on her lips. The aether tie broke as she struggled to breathe, and Sam slumped in the aftermath, sagging against the soaked floor while water raced around her.

His arms slipped beneath her as Nat attempted to find firm footing and leverage enough to raise her out of the wet.

Sam grabbed hold of him and forced her feet underneath her, grateful she'd torn enough strips from her skirt that it didn't tangle around her calves.

"I'm okay now," she shouted into his ear, only remembering Mister Garth's presence too late.

But if the engineer heard her, he said nothing from the other side of the pipes where he worked at keeping the fire lit despite the water sloshing around their feet and the unsteady surface.

Nat pulled her in close to say, "I have to check for other pipes. Are you sure you'll be fine?"

The thought of reaching for the aether made a chill race up her spine, or maybe that was only the air drying her clothes. Still, she knew her help could make the difference between survival and drowning. "I'll work this side of the pipes."

"You know how?" He frowned at her, his eyes narrowed in sudden suspicion.

Sam offered a weak smile. "I was listening…earlier." She lifted the torn edge of her skirt. "I've been doing what I can."

Nat gaped at her for a while, seemingly struck dumb at the glimpse of leg he might have seen when she showed him the source of her cloth strips. What he would have said next, she didn't know, because the ship sank on one side, throwing her at him in a most undignified manner.

His hold was gentle as he set her to rights, but the moment had broken and their friendship restored.

"Have some of my strips. You'll need your clothing for warmth as much as covering."

Sam laughed. "Who will see me anyway?"

If he could have turned a darker shade of red, she knew his skin would have at her careless words. She thrust a hand blindly toward him, a plea for the canvas and to have her words forgotten.

He seemed as grateful to comply as she was that he did.

The rough canvas texture filled her palm, and Sam curled her fingers around the ties. "We'll manage."

She couldn't tell which of them she tried to comfort and doubted Nat could have heard her whisper anyway as he set out to check the pipes too close to the engineer for her to follow. Sam saw him join Mister Garth before awareness returned.

Whatever her confusion, she had no time to waste, especially since she didn't dare risk connecting with the aether. She'd have to check the pipes as Nat did, inspecting each joint and running a hand along the length where it didn't burn too hot in the hopes of feeling a vibration before it became strong enough to tear the fixture free.

Nat caught glimpses of Samantha through the pipes, but only because he knew what to look for. Mister Garth trusted him to keep the pipes together, or had no choice but to trust. It took all of the engineer's skill to keep the coals lit and steam rising to the challenge of turning gears that threatened to bend and snap every time the ship lurched.

As minutes melted into hours with the storm raging all around them, he didn't think he'd ever worked so hard. Day turned into the longest night he'd known with the storm clouds too thick to let the sun mark the passage of time.

Nat ran from one side to the next, following instinct, sounds heard deep inside him when his ears felt as waterlogged as the floor had become.

Without Samantha taking on the deeper pipes, he'd never have kept them together, and he'd be hard pressed not to let the one word Mister Garth condemned slip off his tongue if they made it through without damage they'd have no hope of repairing.

Then between one moment and the next, they passed beyond the storm's skirt.

He'd grown so accustomed to the bucking floor his feet fought for purchase on the now steady boards. His knees folded under him, and Nat fell with a splash into the brackish liquid still sloshing back and forth in a weak imitation of the storm's fury.

Mister Garth let loose a long sigh, the only sign he'd feared for their safety as much as Nat had. "We'll need to be pumping out this water soon enough so the pipes don't corrode."

Nat didn't realize he'd groaned until the sound echoed against his eardrums as he dragged himself back to his feet. They'd been working straight through with one short break to choke down some bread and hard cheese Jenson sent to feed them.

The engineer laughed with only a short measure of his normal volume. "It can wait. I suspect there'll be much demand for the pump, and the stores most likely have a deeper measure of water. Our hatch is enough to keep out most of it, though from the sound, I'm guessing a pipe's the cause of our damp feet, is it not?"

A nod ended deeper than Nat had planned, his eyes shut and chin resting on his chest before he forced it back up. A yawn stretched his face past comfort.

"It's a wonder you were able to set it back in place by yourself, and you kept lord knows how many others from breaking. Go on and find your hammock. You've earned a rest. I'll get some of the others to bail us out."

Nat forced his back to straighten. "I'll do it. You worked as hard as I did, if not harder."

The engineer didn't know that Nat had help in keeping the pipes together, though how he'd explain ties made from printed cloth instead of sail he did not know. All the more reason to keep the task of scooping up this water from falling to another's hands.

Mister Garth crossed to his side and closed a firm hand on Nat's shoulder. "Your willingness speaks well of you, but it's not like this engine's never seen water before. We both need a rest, and I can't say I'm all that pleased to bring a bunch of clumsy sailors down here. It can keep. The captain's sure to have other work for those few who rested through the storm as much as the pump. When the ship's secured is soon enough to get her engine chamber set to rights. Who knows what mischief the sailors might get up to if left down here on their own?"

The engineer could dismiss Nat's weak laugh as a consequence of the exhaustion, but really it came because the mischief others might come to had little in common with Mister Garth's worries. Samantha would be hard pressed to hide if the engine room swarmed with sailors eager to see as much as possible in a rare chance to lay their eyes on a space usually kept barred to them.

"Come on, Mister Bowden." The engineer clapped him on the back with enough force to send Nat staggering toward the steps. "There'll be work for the both of us soon enough. Best not to waste what hours we can claim in our hammocks. I've doused the fire already so no more harm can come to our engine before we check her state more completely. The captain will have to take bearings with that faulty gadget he swears by anyway. Our steam-driven paddles may have carried us beyond the fury of the storm, but I doubt the turbulent water did as well in keeping us on course."

Nat nodded a response again, too tired to formulate words with any bit of sense in them.

When they reached the hatch, he glanced back down into the darkness, hoping Samantha could find some way to rest herself, a way that didn't mean standing or lying in the chill water. But he had no chance to check on her, not with Mister Garth urging him out, and it wasn't as though he could offer her his hammock.

She'd done well enough on her own down there even before he'd learned of her presence. She had proved time and again to be stronger than he could have imagined. If any way of finding warmth and comfort could be had, she would manage it.

Nat fell asleep the moment his head found woven rope, and though the ship must have been bustling with every manner of activity in the aftermath of the storm, he did not stir until Hassan shook him awake.

"Mister Bowden, they want you on deck. Mister Garth, he's gone impatient to clear his room."

From one blink to the next, Nat found his feet and his sleep-filled brain came alert. "The pump's been freed up?"

Hassan shrugged as he swung into his own hammock, clearly more interested in catching some sleep than answering any questions. He must have been one of those pumping the excess liquid from below deck from the state of his trousers, the damp cloth not enough of a bother to strip before crashing. His snores followed Nat up the steps onto a blindingly bright deck.

"There you are, Mister Bowden. I thought you were leaving me to the work on my own." Mister Garth showed no sign of the wearing storm as he waved Nat over.

Nat rubbed a hand across his face, blinked the sleep from his eyes, and strode over to the engineer, back straight with an effort to look awake. "I'm here and ready."

Mister Garth face creased into a slight smile. "So you are. Take hold of that end of the pump. I wasn't about to let them gawkers in far enough to place the machine. They can lay the pipes to the rail."

The pump, a simple foot-driven mechanism that drove water from one end out the other, had a good heft to it, but Nat had helped clear below decks before and bent to the task properly. Navigating the steps with Mister Garth on the other side proved a challenge, but they managed, knowing they'd reached the floor when their feet splashed down.

"Bring it over here," Mister Garth directed with a nod to the coal bin. The raised edges would offer a safe space over dumping the pump down into the same water it had to remove.

As soon as they'd shifted the pump so three lengths of strong wood offered a solid base, Nat splashed his way to the steps and up them without waiting for the engineer's command. He gathered up enough of the pipe and joins to send the water up on deck, wondering if these pipes could serve the engine in a pinch.

The thought soon vanished under the realization that no sailor would agree to cannibalize the pump, not even for the chance to steam through a storm. Water was both boon and bane to a sailor, a man more comfortable with waves rushing beneath the wood than on solid land while the slosh above boards signaled a horrible, slow death.

Nat caught no sight of Samantha as he alternated with Mister Garth to keep the pressure on the water so it went up the stairs and out the hatch. The foot pedal proved more difficult to pump by hand, but it would be worse to take the water out one bucketful at a time. Still, he couldn't help the sigh of relief that escaped when Mister Garth caught his arm to stop his up and down surges.

"Enough hard labor for you, Mister Bowden? And here I thought you were made of sterner stuff."

About to protest, Nat caught sight of the engineer's grin and recognized a weariness in the other man to match his own. "It's just this task is normally shared by a handful."

"And the pump isn't usually set so high above the floor. Trust me when I say I know. I started out where you are now a long time before. The engine room isn't supposed to get so much water in, and it wouldn't have if her pipes weren't as old and worn as the rest of her."

Nat gave a tired nod, not bothering to point out the lack of hands had nothing to do with the engine's age. He had his own reasons for keeping prying sailors out of the space and appreciated whatever drove the engineer to do so. "What do we need to do next?"

"You," Mister Garth said, giving him a gentle shove to the door, "are wanted on deck. A measure of sunshine should do you good. I'll get the pump set for carrying out when there's a need."

Though the thought of what awaited him above gave little comfort to his sore muscles, Nat had missed the sunshine. Any more time down in the engine room, and he'd be too pale to stand under the noonday light without ending up on the surgeon's table, thrashing with sun fever.

At the top of the stairs, he glanced back. "Is there anything you want me to fetch you?"

Mister Garth laughed. "I'll make do. I think you'll find Mister Trupt has more of a need. This place still has to dry out before we can do any testing of the engine herself. I figure to poke among the gears and see what damage I find, but I'm not planning to fire up the coals or make her turn the paddles any time soon."

Nat stepped free of the stairs just as the engineer added, "Don't close down the hatch now, Mister Bowden. What the sun can't finish off, you'll have to, crawling through the pipes with a rag."

The threat would have made him tremble before coming to know the engineer better. Now, Nat just laughed.

But he made sure to lock the braces on the hatch so it wouldn't come closed. Just because the threat hadn't been meant to harm didn't mean it wouldn't still be his task, and one he'd have to accept no matter how sore his body what with Samantha hiding somewhere in the maze of metal tubes.

"Ah, there you are, Mister Bowden. I was starting to wonder if you'd been sucked into the pump and thrown overboard." Mister Trupt seemed in a better mood than Nat could remember seeing for a long while.

"No, sir. Just took a bit longer with only the two of us."

The first mate clapped Nat on the shoulder hard enough to send him stumbling forward before a firm hold on his arm caught him. "No doubt, and you're probably sore from top to waterlogged toes. I have no cure for the soreness, but some time up in the ropes will dry you out well enough."

"Yes, sir." Nat made no attempt to control his grin as he headed toward the rigging. He hadn't realized just how much he missed seeing across the waters and the companionship of the other riggers until then.

"Watch your footing," Mister Trupt called after him, humor rippling through his tone.

Nat didn't care. Let them laugh at his enthusiasm. Had his mother her way, he'd be stuck behind the fire in a belching iron carriage, trapped on rails and forced to follow the same exact route. Instead, he had a ship's length to stretch his legs, rope to climb, and new horizons to admire when he wasn't learning the inner workings of the engine, or the heart as Mister Garth liked to call the collection of gears and pipes.

13

N at had barely put hands and feet onto the rigging before he was greeted with a chorus of hallos. Hassan still slept below, but the riggers swinging from the ropes as they checked for frays or unraveling knots all took a moment to give him a smile or call out to him. He felt as though he were a prodigal son, an impression only strengthened when Phil left his post to come to Nat's side.

"I wondered how long that dark hole could keep you. Seems to me you have a knack for the ropes, and a liking for the kiss of the sun." The rigger leaned back, supported by one hand and a bent knee slung over a rope. The sun glistened on his sweat-soaked bare chest.

Nat copied the movement, remembering a time in the heart of the storm when he'd wondered if the sun would ever warm him again.

Neither of them stayed long though. There remained a lot of rope to check, and they didn't want a telling off from Mister Trupt. A good man, and one Nat liked to consider a friend, the first mate played no favorites when it came to keeping the ship in her best form, and her crew swift and sure.

Sometime later, the work no less hard than when he toiled below, but the minutes passing swifter in the fresh air, Phil waved him up to the crow's nest.

"Captain's trying to get our bearings," the rigger told Nat when he climbed the last stretch and swung into the wooden bucket. "You've got one of the sharpest pair of eyes we have, so I want you looking for anything the captain can use."

Nat grabbed hold of the mast, his other hand shading his eyes as he began to scan for any hint of land or formation to match with the charts.

He saw nothing.

Open ocean stretched far in every direction. Not even a gathering of birds hinted that something might be beyond the horizon.

"Anything?" came Mister Trupt's call from below.

Nat shook his head, concentrating too much for a verbal answer.

Phil relayed the absence of a sign, his call followed closely on by the captain's curse, not at the information but at the contraption he swore could find their place on the ocean with no more guide than a steady hand.

Nat suppressed his smile, thinking on the gentle humor that would pass among the sailors in the night as the first mate took proper bearings from the stars.

The professor had a liking for mechanical objects supposed to perform all sorts of miracles, but a real sailor swore by the tried and true. Nat planned to follow in the footsteps of one like Mister Trupt, wanting the respect of his crew when he earned one. Captain Paderwatch had gained only amused tolerance, a reaction so strong it hid the captain's true value and left sailors crediting luck as the reason for their good fortune. Maybe they went so far as to consider the captain a human charm, but nothing more.

"I guess we're fortunate the captain sent you on to the shipyard, Mister Bowden, rather than going himself."

Nat glanced away from his work, eyes sore from the endless staring, and looked instead at Phil. "What do you mean?"

he asked before realizing the rigger had to be referring to the parts he'd won from the shipyard. Mister Garth's warning about too much emphasis put on the shipyard purchases crossed his mind too late to call back the words.

Phil jerked his chin to where the captain still struggled with the contraption. The man did not even bother to glance up and see the featureless ocean surrounding them.

"If he'd gone, we'd have been floundering in the heart of the storm still. The engine couldn't be trusted before those miracle parts, but at least it worked some of the time, not like that thing the captain bought to guide us."

"Thank heavens for Mister Trupt," Nat said, putting extra emphasis on the name in the hopes of distracting Phil.

"We all know better than that. An open ocean storm has nothing to stop it from getting bigger and stronger. Any hope of survival comes in finding yourself on the slim edge, not with those winds bearing straight down on you like it was. With the sails in to protect the cloth, we'd have been nothing more than a scrap of wood on the surface…for as long as we kept afloat. That engine sure saved us all."

Nat glanced toward the hatch only to see Mister Garth coming up for a stretch. "The engine did. And it's been working strong ever since Mister Garth did the last repairs. He can do wonders with decent parts. I'm glad I was able to lend a hand."

Phil shook his head. "I see what you're doing there. You can say whatever you will, but we know the truth. That engine skipped and lurched its way across the water, as likely to jerk us off our path as push us on it. Only one thing changed, Mister Bowden, and that thing was you."

Nat shrugged and leaned out over the other side of the crow's nest, pretending to focus on something in the distance.

He could do no good by arguing. It would only fix the idea more firmly in the man's mind, and make it that much more likely for Phil to convince the rest. The engineer seemed to have let go of his angst about the shipyard events, but having the riggers push his face into it once again would do little to keep Mister Garth's good mood intact.

After his next two comments were ignored, Phil turned his attention back to the horizon, but neither he nor Nat found any hint of land. Wherever they were, the best they could use on the charts would be a space with no features at all. Nat strained to see anything to mark their bearing but the water ran too deep for visible currents and the birds gave no hope of a change as they made their way forward.

Miracles brought with them dangers, especially when he had secrets not his own to keep, but he couldn't help remembering the few times he'd glanced over while pumping out the water to see Mister Garth at work on the engine. From what he'd observed, and the jarring sound of the engineer's hammer, he didn't think the new repairs showed the same brilliance as what had been there when first he was allowed into the engine room.

Nat cursed under his breath, but loud enough to attract a questioning glance from Phil. He shook off the attention at the same time as his wayward thoughts. Mister Garth had had as little sleep since the storm began as any of them. Why would he show the same skill as coming off a quiet voyage and rest on shore?

Now Nat seemed the one infected by a belief in miracles.

14

"That's the last of it, I'm thinking," Mister Garth said as he and Nat climbed out of the engine chamber toward the end of the day.

After the midday meal, Nat had gone back to help Mister Garth scrape collected salt from the valves and everywhere else it had built up once the heat from the sun dried away most of the water that carried the dusty minerals.

"On any other voyage, I'd wait until we found port to wash the salt out with river water," the engineer said as he wiped his fingers on the legs of his trousers, "But then, there's never supposed to be this much loose water in here either."

He glanced back toward Nat as he mounted the steps, and a protest started to form on Nat's lips before he realized Mister Garth's gaze went beyond him to the pipes. All too many of their joints had weakened and worn to the point of needing canvas to hold them together. He should know, having wrapped them himself, those Samantha hadn't gotten to first.

"In the next port, we'll get more pipes and fixtures," he said, meaning to reassure.

Mister Garth laughed once. "It would surprise me not at all if you got the captain to refit the whole of them, young Bowden." He paused, a hand on the nearest support holding the hatch open. "But that's not where my worry lies. Between the new damage and the pipes, if we hit another storm of significance…"

Nat remembered his thoughts about the engineer's abilities then dismissed them. With only so many spare parts for the engine, and none at all for the pipes, Mister Garth had reason to worry. Fresh or weary, a man could only do so much without supplies.

A ship as old as theirs was usually kept to the shorter passages, the continent shores, or maybe into the Mediterranean. He suspected Professor Paderwatch's hand in this destination.

Little fortune lay on the well-traveled routes they'd been assigned before, as much trade done on foot and wagon as ever on the waters. But their captain knew the way to security lay in risk. He'd told Nat so many a time. And what greater risk than charging off across a wide ocean to destinations limited to the ships making that treacherous passage.

Sometimes, though, it seemed as much the need to see new vistas drove the captain as any thought of profit. Weighing the risks sat on an altered scale in his hands.

"Eh." Mister Garth shrugged, jerking Nat from his worries. "Don't listen to an old man's grumbles. She's a fine engine. She's saved us once on this voyage and will again. We just have to give her some care, and she'll be as good as she ever was." He freed the hatch and stepped halfway out. "But for now, I heard from Jenson the captain called for a keg to be brought up from below. Seems he thinks the crew deserves a little something extra with supper after all the hard work we put in. You'll get a fair measure, I'm sure."

Nat doubted that.

The captain may have released him from his lessons in the interests of the crew, but the professor was unlikely to risk a telling off from Nat's mother, who had drawn out a promise of moderation when Nat had finally convinced her, a promise she'd extracted from the professor as well. She'd allowed for watered ale, but never anything stronger. "I'll be grateful for a splash," he muttered.

"That's the way of it? Have you ever tasted the fiery stuff?"

As much as he wanted to pretend to have been like every other sailor on the boat, Nat shook his head. He kept enough hidden from the engineer without lying to save face, and he doubted his absence from the line had passed unnoticed by the crew for all they forbore to tease him for it.

Mister Garth clapped a hand on Nat's shoulder and drew him the rest of the way out of the engine room, letting the hatch fall with a solid thump. "That's something we'll have to see about. A man works as hard as you have, on the ropes and in the dark, he deserves a little consideration. I'll give you a slug from my own glass if that's all you have the chance of. Not even a true apprentice, and you've the spirit of one ready to learn anything. Better still, you're ready to listen to those with more experience. I misjudged you back then, thinking you another of those society boys thrust on us with no intent to do more than reap a portion of our earnings. The others said no, but I wouldn't listen until you proved yourself many times over. Yes, for that alone you deserve a measure of grog, and a measure you'll have."

Together they marched right up to where Mister Trupt was serving out the prize though Nat would rather have stood aside. He knew what he'd face at the top of the line, knew his mother's word had more sway than anything he offered even though he'd become a man grown since she'd extracted her promise. Still, better the engineer see for himself than to believe Nat a coward.

The sailors in front of them moved out of the way one after another as they accepted their measure, but they didn't go far. Jenson had brought his big stew pot up on deck and eve-ryone gathered round, well placed to witness his humiliation.

By the time their turn came, Nat's stomach had soured. He thought maybe it would have been better to step aside for all that the men might see him as acting too grand for their sim-ple spirits, but he'd missed his chance.

A frown pinched the skin between Mister Trupt's eyes when his glance took in Nat's position next to the engineer.

Nat braced himself, ready for the first mate's quiet com-mand to leave the grog to those who deserved it.

Mister Garth strode forward before anything could be said. "A full tot for my young apprentice here. He's worked his fin-gers to the bone for this ship, above and below her decks, and no one should deny him what he deserves."

Mister Trupt turned his calm gaze on the engineer, no sign of the surprise he must have felt marking his expression, first at Mister Garth's good humor and second that Nat would be the object of same.

"Well?" The engineer widened his stance and propped fists on both hips, his stature still nothing compared to the muscled first mate.

A slight smile curled Mister Trupt's lip on one side. "Not too long ago, you'd have been standing in his way." He held up a hand to still Mister Garth's protest. "It's good to see the crew working together, and working hard. It's what a strong ship needs, and why this barrel came up from the hold after all."

The engineer's shoulders relaxed and his hands fell to his sides. "So you'll give the boy what's coming to him?"

Nat knew it wouldn't be so easy, a fact shown when Mister Trupt shook his head.

"No. I have orders about the boy. Orders from the captain that I'm not inclined to stick my neck out to deny."

Nat put a hand on Mister Garth's arm. He appreciated the engineer's support, especially after all that had passed between them, but this battle they could not win, and there would be others better worth the effort.

The first mate had glanced away, reaching behind him for a rough mug to serve up a measure for the next sailor in line. Nat would have taken the moment to step out of the line and prevent more humiliation, but he didn't know what Mister Garth would do if he did. He couldn't leave the engineer to suffer for his mother's proscriptions.

Mister Trupt turned the tap for less time than he had for the other sailors, a sign he'd taken Mister Garth's rebellion poorly. The engineer wouldn't have enough to share even if he still felt willing.

"I have orders about the boy," the first mate repeated as though he had not paused at all, "But I see no boy here."

Nat's attention jerked from the mug to the man's face then back to the mug as it was thrust toward him. He barely had time to wrap his fingers around it before Mister Trupt let go.

"I see only a bunch of pungent sailors and a young man well on the way to making something of himself."

Cheeks aching with the force of his grin, Nat reached out to shake the first mate's hand, forgetting the mug in his excitement.

Mister Trupt steadied his grasp. "Go easy on that. It's never so strong as your first tot, and the pain that comes from it neither." Despite the admonishment, the first mate returned Nat's smile before selecting another mug for Mister Garth and topping it off.

The engineer threw an arm around Nat's shoulders and together they marched over to Jenson and the steaming pot, Mister Garth beaming as though he'd brought Nat up to this moment all by himself. The man's delight made up for any consequences that might come of this adventure and eased the slight guilt for denying his mother. She didn't know how it was out here, and best she never find out. A little of the strong spirits was the least of his encounters, and one unlikely to cause lasting harm.

15

With steaming bowls of stew and a mug of grog each, Mister Garth and Nat crossed the deck to a space a little away from the rest before they settled. Nat never considered leaving the engineer to a quiet meal until too late, but the man seemed happy for the company.

"I may have convinced Mister Trupt to see you as something other than a boy, but I'll not be the one to dump you in amongst the crew's drunken revels. Nor will I take you up on the bow and chance you flipping the rail. There won't be much done on the next watch would be my guess."

The engineer took a big swallow from his mug, but Nat remembered the first mate's warning and poured a cautious sip into his mouth. He gasped and choked, the grog burning its way across his tongue and down his throat, to rest warm and comforting in his belly.

"You're a good man, Mister Bowden, for all your family comes from the big houses," Mister Garth said, his voice a little louder and no sign of his grumpy nature. "Can't trust those big houses, no siree. They would like to sit on their thrones while the likes of us do all the work, but they're quick enough to take credit where it isn't due. Not you, though, Mister Bowden. Not you. You speak the truth like a command from God, holding to it even when a lie might do you better. 'I didn't take them,' you said, and I didn't have the worth to recognize yours."

The normally surly and short-spoken engineer had faded as they'd been working together, but with each tip of the mug, that man seemed even farther away.

Instead of enjoying the change, Nat felt his shoulders tighten with every jolly word.

If Mister Garth could see into his head, he'd know Nat kept much from him, lies of omission as heavy as the truths he'd maintained when wrongfully charged.

Nat wiped a hand across his sweaty forehead before raising his own mug to stop the secrets he kept from spilling off his tongue.

Mister Garth didn't seem to notice the lack of response, barely pausing to take a bite of stew between words.

"Never thought I'd share the engine room again after my last apprentice cost me a ship. If not for Captain Paderwatch, I might never have gotten another, at least not as an engineer."

"Captain says he looks for potential," Nat said. "Or at least that's what he told me. Even my mother's urgings wouldn't have made him take me on otherwise."

The engineer raised his mug only to shrug and cast it down upon finding it empty. "Tied close to the apron strings were you? Explains the lack of grog, it sure does. Mothers just can't understand the ways of the sea, especially not the big house mothers. But you're not like other big house folk, you and the captain. Something special."

Nat pushed his empty bowl aside, heat flushing his face. "What do you have against the big houses as you call them, anyway?"

"Them big house leeches aren't better than me, but they're quick to act as though being in their presence is a privilege. I'll tell you just how wonderful they are. You listen up right, boy."

Bristling at the diminished title and the slander of his family, Nat struggled to his feet only to find the deck oddly sloped. He sank back in a graceless tumble then tried to put his elbows under him to pretend he'd meant to lie down instead. At least the engineer seemed more focused on the mast behind Nat's shoulder than on his troubles.

"My former ship, now there was a beauty. Everything tip top shape, fresh boards beneath our feet, and the metal gearing so new it shone. All polished up, you see. As an engineer, I had hardly to do a thing to keep her engine running. And if something failed, I had more than enough spares to swap out. Got a reputation for skill based on how long her paddles cleaved the water, and a rare day came when I had to take her down."

Nat stopped fighting the deck, settling in to listen as he'd been bade. The man said nothing more against Nat's family, after all, and any tidbit about an engine was worthy of his attention.

Mister Garth fumbled for his mug before sighing when he remembered he'd downed his ration. "They assigned me an apprentice. Thought I could teach the young man how to keep an engine running clean. Back then I could do no wrong. A line of men would have formed if given the chance. Instead, the captain brought me some educated fellow. Thought he knew everything when he'd barely stepped foot on a deck, much less below one."

Nat rolled to his side, wondering if he should protest, but then he'd met enough among the sons of his parents' friends to recognize the type. Not worth the effort to defend.

"I taught that young man. I taught him everything I knew, or I tried to when he chose to listen. Never realized how he planned to get his name made. Never knew he thought my beauty of a ship should be his own."

Caught up in the story, Nat could do no more than whisper, "What happened then?"

Mister Garth needed no encouragement to continue. Whether he even heard Nat or remembered he had an audience was in question from the way the engineer focused on the distance, his eyes viewing a sour past rather than anything another could see.

"That young man spent his time among his peers. Not the likes of us real sailors for him. And he put the word in the captain's ear, told the first mate and all the officers, for it was a big vessel with four full masts—not that they counted for much under my care. He told them I did nothing. Spent all day snoozing beneath my hatch when others—namely him—were working. Said if I'd known a lick about engines, the knowledge must have drained out of my ears some time since, and only his book learning kept the engine running smooth."

Nat sat up then, ignoring the way his head spun. He knew a thing or two about rumors and false accusations. At least Mister Garth had not done so to harm but rather from misreading circumstances he had no reason to expect.

"That's right, Mister Bowden. My own apprentice sticking a knife between my ribs and wriggling it there until no one among the ranks could trust me. Me, who'd been the talk of the fleet."

"What did you do?"

Mister Garth's gaze snapped to Nat. "What else could I do? I kicked him right out of my engine room a lot of good that did me. Snuck back in when I wasn't about and damaged the pipes way in the back. He knew I'd just inspected the lot and wouldn't be doing so again soon. My sour luck the pipe failed in a storm and the ship damage fell on my head. After all, he'd been barred from the room. Clearly I'd shown myself up as the fraud he'd called me."

The engineer fell silent, his brows lowered into a scowl and any sign of the earlier good humor gone.

Nat stared down at his hands, the reason for Mister Garth's reticence laid out before him. After an experience like that, why would the man trust again? That apprentice had cost the engineer everything, and had done so maliciously, deliberately. But a thread of worry snaked through Nat as he wondered if his actions would seem any better should they come to light.

Once again, lies stood between the engineer and the one he'd let into the engine room. Mister Garth had no ties to Samantha, and no reason to put the well-being of a stowaway over that of the ship.

Nat had no way of knowing how the engineer would react to the truth, and the risk to Samantha hadn't changed. Had they gone to the captain when he'd first discovered her, things might have been different, but now he'd lose any respect he'd earned, and just might join in her punishment.

But how could he break the engineer's trust, knowing what he now knew? Doing the right thing had never seemed more difficult than in that moment.

His head started to pound and his stomach to roil as he weighed the needs of Samantha against the betrayal of Mister Garth. For all his reasons were sound, he couldn't prove Mister Garth's opinion of young men from the big houses false, not when he practiced a deceit as great as the man's first apprentice.

The last stood out in his aching head.

Whatever the consequences, he'd find a way to protect Samantha but he could not lie to Mister Garth any longer.

Nat twisted around to speak to the engineer, his mouth already open to release the first word, when a loud snore drowned out anything he might have said.

Mister Garth no longer sat upon the deck. Instead, the engineer sprawled out, no thought to dignity or pride, fast asleep.

For just one instant, Nat thought he should shake the man awake and confess, but the urge passed. They'd been working hard. Mister Garth needed his sleep, and like as not, he'd get none with the truth cast between them.

A yawn split Nat's face as the deck no longer seemed so uninviting. He lay down once more and pillowed his head on one arm before sinking into oblivion.

16

*M*orning made its presence known with stabs of light in Nat's face. He rolled over to escape, only to find no relief. The sun's rays came from every side.

A groan issued from another's lips brought Nat to full wakefulness and awareness of his headache. Memory returned, and with it a new understanding of the evils of hard spirits. He sat up, one hand over his eyes, and waited for the world to stop spinning.

"Here. It'll help."

Nat cracked his eyelids up a fraction to see Mister Trupt with a mug, tendrils of steam rising from its surface. He wanted to reject the offer, but one look at the first mate's face, and he took possession of the mug.

Mister Trupt didn't move away. "Drink it up, Mister Bowden. I treated you like a man, but damn me if I'll suffer your moaning for the privilege."

The smell offered little comfort, but with the first mate standing over him, Nat had no choice but to pour it down his gullet and pray it wouldn't taste as bad on the return trip.

To his surprise, the warm liquid felt much like the grog had the night before. Instead of surging back up, it settled his stomach and eased his head until he could open both eyes without feeling the sun's touch as an assault on his senses.

The first mate laughed aloud, reminding Nat of the headache he'd so recently suffered. "That's the way of it, Mister

Bowden. You're a man for truth, and a sailor man too. Took your pleasure and punishment both. Now see what you can do about helping the captain figure out our whereabouts. That engine has never worked so well and has never taken us so far as it did during the storm."

By the time Nat had recovered his feet, Mister Trupt was off rousting the rest of the crew, his treatment rougher for most. The drink might have helped Nat's stomach and head, but the deck movement seemed strange while his knees kept threatening to buckle beneath him.

Nat staggered across the deck to the captain's cabin, not looking forward to the lecture he'd be sure to receive.

"There you are, Nathaniel. I hear you've outgrown your mother's strictures."

Nat mumbled something in reply, but the professor had already turned away to stare at the charts.

"We haven't been down this way since I took over as captain of this vessel, and the readings Mister Trupt provided from the stars show us far off course."

"He blames the engine." Nat moved to the captain's side and stared at the chart as he struggled to make his mind settle.

Captain Paderwatch grunted. "As well he should. But he also knows what to bless for our swift passage through the storm with minimal damage. We could have been floating in the water with only shattered boards to hold us if not for the engine. Never ran as smooth or as well. I didn't expect such results when I forced the two of you together. Well done, my boy."

Nat ducked his head to hide a flush of pleasure at the compliment. "I didn't do all that much."

The captain tapped the chart, his comment already forgotten. "Here. We must be right about here, and yet there should be an island within sight according to this chart. None of the riggers have seen a glimpse of land, nor any evidence of same."

"I didn't see any when I was up there yesterday either." Nat went over the calculations, but everything seemed as it should be. The chart proved the same, so he moved to check the chart books that sometimes had descriptions of the areas.

The captain nodded in approval and went back to whatever he'd been working on once Nat took over the charts. Captain Paderwatch had trouble with the crabbed writing in the chart books, something he'd never admit to, but Nat could recognize the strain from watching his grandfather.

Soon enough, he found an account of the island they couldn't see. While listed on the charts as true land, from the description, it was little more than a sandbar, the spew of a volcano long sunken.

"I'll tell the riggers," Nat said, pausing only enough to stow the book before heading out the door.

"Tell them what?" the captain called after.

Nat almost tripped over his legs as he tried to reverse direction too fast, only then realizing he'd kept his discovery to himself. One hand braced on the doorframe, he leaned in to say, "The island has little profile and no value. No water or growth. They're looking for the wrong sign."

"Excellent."

Nat didn't wait for more or question the captain's approval. Even so small an island meant knowing where they were and so where they needed to go.

17

With the information Nat provided, several of the riggers sighted the bare strip within two bells as the tides shifted enough to reveal it. The captain called out for them to drop anchor nearby and assess the ship further while he decided their path.

"Figures we get the engine working, and it sends us into the middle of nowhere with only that for a landing," one of the deckmen muttered within Nat's hearing.

He turned to protest, but Mister Trupt, with his second sense for trouble, clapped a hand on Nat's shoulder.

"Anything you say will do no good and may cause harm," the first mate said.

Nat shrugged free. "What would you care? You feel much the same. You said so yourself."

"That I'd prefer somewhere with shade and fresh water? Who wouldn't?"

"That you blame the engine."

Mister Trupt pulled Nat to the aft wall where they could see what the chart had marked as an island, though already the rising waters had reduced it to a mere shadow. "You have it in mind to run a ship and a crew someday, but you'll do worse than Captain Paderwatch if you can't feel through to the crew's heart. Tell me, is it better they grumble and gripe about the same engine they'll pray to if a storm comes up, or that they blame the captain for taking us out on deep waters?"

Nat looked from the first mate to the nearest of the crewmen. He could see the tension in their shoulders, and he'd heard Jenson mention how he'd started counting their provisions, deciding how best to stretch some out and which could be tossed in a stew despite the salt water drenching.

He'd never considered that they'd blame the captain, feeling instead their angst at the engine was directed somehow at him.

Mister Trupt slapped him on the back, reading the answer in his face. "There you go, Mister Bowden. We'll make a solid captain out of you after all. Now get on with your task. I believe you were bringing some oil to Mister Garth, were you not?"

"Yes, sir. That I was." Nat lifted the stoppered pot in his hand as a salute and continued across the deck to the engine room hatch.

He mulled on the first mate's words all the way, wondering at the delicate balance between rumor and truth he'd found this voyage to be. No matter how he looked at it, sometimes truth had little to do with right or best, and yet at the same time truth had everything to do with it. The truth of the sailors' having a target other than one likely to incite mutiny outweighed the truth of the engine being their savior rather than a curse. He stumbled on the first step as he realized the truth of Samantha's risk outweighed Mister Garth's need to know about the stowaway just as much. As long as Nat cut his rations to feed her and no one else's.

"Careful there, Mister Bowden. I doubt we'll have a chance to refresh our oil supplies on that sandbar you called an island," Mister Garth said, reaching up from the bottom of the steps to take hold of the clay pot.

"I didn't call it an island," Nat protested, forgetting Mister Trupt's lesson long enough for his tongue to slip free.

Had Mister Garth's good humor remained past the morning, his response might have been different, but the engineer jerked the pot free and scowled at him. "Take responsibility for your words, boy, not like those sailors up there. They blame our beauty of an engine when they should be praising her."

Nat climbed down the stairs and followed Mister Garth deeper, weighing the gain of sharing Mister Trupt's insight against the engineer's reaction to any appearance of schooling. Or worse, giving the man a sense that the first mate manipulated the crew.

"You'd think she didn't suffer any in the storm from how they're talking. That she somehow drove us here of a purpose."

"They're just talking," Nat said after deciding best to offer no reasoning at all.

"Talking nonsense and blather that they are. Don't you go defending them, either. Pretty soon we'll have to bar the hatch to keep them from storming down here and causing even more damage."

"They'd never—"

"You know nothing, boy, and you're getting nothing done neither. Take this rag." He tipped the pot to soak a portion of the rag across its mouth. "Start rubbing down every gear you can reach. Salt can do horrible damage if left to sit."

Nat opened his mouth to accept the task, but Mister Garth just shoved the rag at him and scowled until he took it in silence.

He'd been called "boy" twice since he came back down, enough of a sign the engineer could barely tolerate his presence. With the way Mister Garth let the sailors' words draw out his sour character, whether the engine ran well or poorly, Nat felt even more grateful for Mister Trupt's timely intervention. Better he let their mutters wash over him, and Mister Garth's too. He'd show the engineer his value through hard work, and soon enough they'd be on their way with all this behind them.

18

Mister Garth declared a need for air some hours later, and since the supper bell rang not too long ago, Nat let free a grateful sigh. No matter what, he wouldn't be the first to leave, for all his fingers were slicked with oil and stung wherever he'd sliced himself on sharp edges.

"You coming?"

Nat took the lack of "boy" as a good sign and scrambled free of the back side of the engine. "I'm coming."

"How're the gears looking back there?"

As much as he wanted to respond with some comment about how slippery they were, this time Nat kept his tongue trapped between his teeth long enough for his brain to catch up. "I've cleared some salt, but there's no pitting I could see."

Mister Garth grunted a response and stomped up the steps, clearly without his good humor restored.

Nat could only hope they'd be on their way sooner rather than later, and not just because the sailors' complaints would worsen Mister Garth's disposition. He didn't want to learn how those complaints could turn dark if supplies started running low.

They separated at the kitchen, Mister Garth not commanding his presence, and Nat just as happy to leave him to his own dark cloud.

Nat saw the engineer heading out to the bow in his search for fresh air. He'd be happier for it and had chosen the far side where he wouldn't seethe at the crew's grumbles. Even better, Mister Garth would have no clear sight of the engine room hatch.

Jenson had already cut portions in case getting to civilized land took longer than they hoped, and Nat had been working hard enough to empty his belly. But he knew of another who'd eaten less often, especially with Mister Garth always present and so much to do on the engine.

Nat held the bowl close to his chest as he worked the hatch open without looking, his gaze sweeping the area in the hopes of catching sight of Mister Garth should the engineer return. He stumbled on the first step and almost committed the unforgivable sin of wasting food, even less forgivable when his meager portion went to feed two.

"Samantha," he called, keeping his voice quiet despite the hatch having lowered into place behind him.

The dark pressed down on him as he waited for his eyes to adjust, unwilling to risk the meal a second time. Fear burned harder as Samantha failed to come, then her pale face loomed out of the dark close enough to startle him into jerking back.

"Don't spill it now," she whispered. "It smells so good, but I'm not yet hungry enough to lick it off these salt-splattered boards."

"Who says I came to share it?"

Nat had meant only to tease, but with his eyes becoming accustomed to the dark, he saw the hurt on her face as she turned to head into her corner.

"Wait. I was teasing. I didn't mean it."

The hurt remained from the tension in her shoulders, but she stopped her retreat.

"I'm sorry. I didn't think. For a moment, I didn't think about how it would seem. Please."

Her shoulders relaxed all of a sudden, the breath rushing out of her as she turned again. "No, Nathaniel, I should be sorry. I teased you first. I should have known. Besides, who am I to complain? You worked hard all day, and instead of gulping that down, you brought it to share."

She sounded so reserved, more at home in his mother's parlor than cramped in the engine room half under the first row of pipes, that a laugh escaped Nat's lips. "I'm sorry, you're sorry, but we'll be more so if this stew congeals, and we have to eat it with the fat separated and floating on the top."

Instead of joining his laugh, she only nodded then ducked through the first pipe without waiting for him.

They had an unspoken agreement about not sharing food out in the open, not after Mister Garth came so close to catching them together a day before the storm hit. She never took the bowl from him either, though she showed as much skill with tight spaces as he'd learned up on the ropes. Just as she'd responded so swiftly to his teasing, she took care not to presume. Nat couldn't imagine the life of a young woman that would prepare her so. For all her manners, she'd suffered privation before and had learned to deal with less when most of their class would always expect more even now.

As they huddled over the bowl, each scooping out mouthfuls with a far from adequate piece of bread torn once already by Jenson and now split between the two of them, Nat kept his dips light and chewed each bite a second time to give her the space to eat a fair share.

She ate quickly and quietly, her thick bones showing sharp against her skin, sturdy wrists reduced to little more than a paint smear of flesh color.

Samantha was careful to leave him the greater portion each time, though he wasn't able to bring her something from every meal. That care had begun to show, and he feared for her health, not so much for now as when she left the ship and had no one to watch out for her. She'd proved resourceful, and a good worker if given the chance, but in making her way alone in a strange land he worried she'd never have the opportunity to work before she starved.

"Eat the rest. I'm full up already."

Though she gave him a doubting glance, her hunger over-whelmed any restraint as she pushed the remaining crumbs of her bread into the bowl in an effort to sweep up every last bit of broth. Her desperate movements were sign enough he'd made the right choice, though he had to cough hard to cover the grumbling of his stomach.

Nat refused to have her worry at the cost of his gift. He'd been well fed before and had enough chance to eat still that going shy wouldn't cost him what her limited diet had cost her already. He had little hope that would change after they reached a port where she could slip free and be forever lost to him.

19

The snick of a flint striker made Sam freeze, one hand still pressed to the bottom of Nat's bowl.

They'd failed to notice Mister Garth's arrival. Nat's coughing and an ill-timed cloud must have conspired to cover both the light and noise of the hatch.

A small mew reached her ears before she realized it came from her own throat.

Again, Nat coughed.

His reaction would have caused concern if not for her knowing just why her only friend on this ship forced the sound.

"Mister Bowden? You'll hardly find fresh air down here."

Nat pressed a finger to his lips, took up the bowl, and left her behind as he climbed through the pipes with his usual lack of grace.

From the light spilling ever nearer, Mister Garth had already started toward them, pushing through the smaller pipes with an ease showing long practice.

She wanted to move further into the dark, but fought the impulse. This close, the engineer would catch sight of her movement and she'd be discovered.

Staying still took more strength and energy than building a mechanical ever had. Her muscles ached with the tension while her ears strained as well, trying to pick up every sound, searching for a warning now that the time for warnings had long past.

"I like the rush of water against the hull," Nat said, his voice ringing with conviction despite that not being his true reason for winding through the pipes. Perhaps he spoke the truth after all, if not the full of it.

"You can only hear it now because the engine's quiet. You should be drawn to her beat more than that of the sea. It wants to swallow us whole without leaving any sign we'd ever existed." The engineer's grumble resonated through the enclosed space.

She shuddered at the thought, true for her more than any other. If the ship failed them, at least their families would know to mourn when they never came to shore. She'd been listed on the passenger manifest of another vessel, this one taking on no passengers, and only Nat knew of her presence here.

The shadows from the lantern swung over her, the edge of light coming much too close for comfort, but its progress stopped when Nat met the engineer before he could come any further.

"What's that in your hand?"

The engineer's question made Sam wonder as well before she realized even as Mister Garth continued, "You bringing food down here with you? You better not be calling any rats. We have enough trouble with the salt without rats gnawing through the straps we use to fix the pipes."

Sam glanced to just one of those repairs near where Nat and the engineer stood. Her eyes widened, but she managed to swallow her gasp as she realized what held the pipes together in that spot. A desperate prayer ran through her mind, one that went unanswered as Mister Garth reached up to tug on one of the straps she'd tied before Nat gave her the canvas.

"Eh? What's this?"

The light spilled a wider circle as Mister Garth explored what his fingers had already discovered.

In the gift of deeper shadow, she finally was able to shift further away, but it would make no difference. Once the source of those strips of cloth came known, she would be revealed, her attempt to help dooming her as surely as the way she'd sped the engine of the coach assigned to take her to the dock for her ship to the Continent.

"It's nothing," Nat said, his words rushed. "I tore some strips from my shirt to secure the joint."

"Are shirts so easy for you to come by then?" the engineer growled. "And of such fine weave. You're a fool if you think you can afford the like on a sailor's pay. Or does your family support you still, this just a jaunt for you, a game with the chance of some extra pocket money? You think to be one of us when you throw away what others would pay a pretty penny to possess if they had a shiny enough coin to afford such."

Sam cringed, knowing Nat took this abuse in her name, just as he'd risked his very life when she'd been reduced to the existence of a rat.

Where she expected a tremble, Nat's voice came across firm and clear. "I admit I thought little of it. The pipes were necessary to keep us afloat and moving out of the storm. A shirt seemed a small sacrifice."

Mister Garth grunted, and the shadows changed, a sign he'd started out of the pipes that had become her refuge, one so easily breached.

"So you're wasteful and a fool. Better to have climbed free of the pipes and got more strips of sail canvas. It's twice as strong if not half as pricey. You're lucky those sloppy repairs held through the storm, but I'm not chancing my life and the rest of the crew on the quality of your cloth. There's torn sail in the far corner. Take it up on deck. I want the sail cut into clean strips no shorter than the length of my arm. And when you're done, you'll climb back in amongst the pipes and fix every one of your repairs. You might be willing to lay odds they'll hold, but the rest of us know better."

"Yes, sir." This time a tinge of resentment colored Nat's tone, and Sam couldn't blame him, yet it was her actions he suffered for and none of his own.

Nat had reached the bottom of the stair when the engineer called him back with, "And take your dirty dish back up to Jenson. Rats, boy. Remember, you gain nothing in making your tale of rats into a truth, and it could cost us all."

His feet stomped the boards a little harder on the way back, but soon the hatch opened.

Sam used the sound of his exit to cover her own passage back to the wall, her hands shaking. A little faster through the pipes, the light a little brighter, and she'd have been revealed. If only her luck could hold through the rest of this voyage and see her safely to another shore. Whether she could find other Naturals across this distance remained to be seen, but if she were discovered here, her life would be forfeit with none to protest except maybe Nat, further risking his position and the respect of the crew for her when she was nothing more than a stowaway for all she'd lived a good life at Henry's hand.

20

The captain demanded Nat's presence over breakfast, undermining his hope to spend the meal with Samantha. Instead, while eating, they'd poured over the charts for this area, returning again and again to the island that wasn't.

"If the charts can't be trusted," Nat asked, "Then how do we find a safe shore?"

Professor Paderwatch glowered not at Nat but at the offending parchment spread before them. "With luck and a prayer. If I could get my gadget working, we wouldn't have to depend on a lazy chart. As it is, with fierce storms like the one we just passed through, I'm doubly concerned with trusting them. I could steer us right into a coral reef, or seek fresh water on something no better than this one." He rubbed a hand over his balding head. "If only I could go back to the times of sitting in a classroom, teaching about all the different peoples on our good earth. Even seeking them under the sure command of a true captain."

"They don't blame you," Nat said with confidence.

After all, they blamed the engine.

"I know all about that blame. It won't last if I can't get us back on course, and I lack the courage to strike out unguided. I was never that man. I decide our path based on knowledge and understanding. A risk, if any, is calculated to its optimum success."

Nat had never seen the professor look so desolate. "There is always risk."

"No, my boy, there is not always risk. Had I kept us in the short paths between England and the Continent, we wouldn't be stranded way out here with limited provisions and no sign of where to get more. I calculated the storm into my decision, but never once thought the engine would perform so well, new parts or no. It's nothing short of miraculous, and not all miracles work in our favor. Just look at the Naturals for proof of that. An amazing ability tied with such lack of control that it becomes worthless." He slapped the table. "As worthless as these charts. Whoever recorded them clearly had eyes on the next place and none for this one, empty as it has proved to be. No job worth doing is worth doing poorly. Remember that Nathaniel. Remember that if you ever have the chance to learn from this disaster."

"You'll figure something out. You've done so time and again, Captain. We'll come out of this with coin in our pockets and a handful of new stories to tell."

"Captain. Professor was always more to my liking, but you do well to remind me of my responsibilities. And I'm keeping you from yours. Go on then, Mister Bowden. If the charts can't be trusted, I'll get my device working. I have no choice."

Though they'd finished the work on the engine and waited only word to turn her back on, Nat accepted the excuse to leave. The captain had been too absorbed in his own troubles to notice Nat's failure to eat his bread.

The day burned hot on his back as he crossed to the engine room, a warning they'd have an uncomfortable time until sundown with the hour so early.

Even the engineer had unbent enough to go barefoot, the press of leather boots and cloth too much for the temperature. At least Mister Garth would be unlikely to hang around the engine room in these conditions, though Samantha would suffer for it.

"Mister Garth?" Nat called, caution winning over eagerness, especially with yesterday's close call.

Samantha came from between the pipes, just as eager for his presence it seemed. "He's not down here this morning. Have you finished the repairs? Will we soon be on our way again?"

Nat dismissed the thought that she'd been missing him, her questions answer enough as to why she'd come forward so quickly.

She was eager only to put this voyage behind her. He couldn't find it in him to blame her for that, which made it all the harder to tell her the truth, the captain's strain foremost in his mind.

"I brought you something to eat," he told her instead. "It's not much, but I spent the morning in the captain's cabin, and he'd have noticed if I failed to touch my food." Nat wondered if that had been true, all things considered, but he couldn't take the chance, not now, not ever. Samantha would remain his secret long after she'd slipped away on foreign docks never to be seen again.

She took the bowl, empty save for the bread and what little porridge had clung to it, but paused before raising the offering to her lips. "And what did you learn?"

Nat sank down on the step. She had noticed his attempt to distract and hadn't been fooled by it.

Samantha shook her head once. "It's not safe to be out here. You can tell me in the pipes."

"Mister Garth isn't likely to come down here on such a hot day, not with our work done and the fire still cold." Even as he said the words, Nat moved past her into the shelter of the pipes.

The delay made his words no less harsh, but they gave him a moment to enjoy her company. He could go without seeing the pain in her face at the knowledge of a longer wait on even shorter rations than the crew. Whatever their complaints, Samantha would spend the time locked down here in the hot engine room with nothing but his infrequent visits to look forward to. She'd suffer the most of all of them.

Samantha settled with her back to the hull and the bowl on the loose cloth between her crossed legs. He mimicked her posture, but said nothing as she raised the bread to her lips, nibbling off tiny bites that she chewed well before swallowing. Another sign she'd suffered this before, extending the meal as long as she could to trick her stomach about its volume. He'd only had to warn her the once.

He half expected her to wave a hand for him to speak then realized that would chance a crumb falling outside the trap of her skirt and skittering under the pipes. He'd never seen her waste food since her first, desperate hunger, a wise choice considering their circumstances. Still, the tension in her shoulders told him she awaited the answer, and after being discovered here yesterday, it wouldn't be wise to linger too long below deck. With the engine room already heating and only growing more uncomfortable, his presence would surely raise questions he couldn't answer.

Nat let out a sigh, knowing he could delay no longer. "The captain's charts are shoddy. We know where we are to a fashion, but we can't trust the markings to show us where more fresh water can be found. The captain doesn't want to set us adrift with no direction, but staying here isn't an option either."

A frown creased the space between her eyes, but she said nothing, only continued to nibble in silence.

"He'll figure something out. The professor's smart. He knows things no one else does."

"The professor?" she mumbled.

Nat shrugged. "That's what he was before assigned to be captain. And it's helped us out before. He's got some gadget…if he can get it to work."

Her gaze jerked to his, fever bright for a moment before she blinked and looked away.

It took so little to raise her hopes, and Nat wanted to make sure her light never dimmed. He'd do whatever he could, even if that meant figuring out the device himself. Maybe he could use some of what he'd learned from the engine to fix it. Gears were gears, and he'd had a much closer look at the workings than he'd expected what with oiling the salt from them.

Nat rose so quickly he had to jerk away from the pipe above his head. "I'll go help him. Don't worry."

"Wait."

He'd already started back toward the hatchway when her call pulled him up short. A glance back showed her holding out the bowl he'd forgotten and something that would raise notice if it went missing. He returned for it, not expecting her to rise until every crumb in her skirt had been captured and consumed.

"Thank you for this. I'd have my hide whipped if it went missing."

She flinched for him, but he shook his head and laughed, caught up in the possibility he could make the professor's gadget work well enough to get them all out of there. "I didn't mean it. The worst I'd face is a tongue lashing from Jenson. We have few enough spares against breakage, and I'd be the one kept waiting if we had to share the dishes. I'll try to come back later, when they give out our water rations. There wasn't enough liquid in that tiny bit of porridge to quench the thirst of a mouse."

"Or a rat," Samantha said, her pixie smile showing she'd heard Mister Garth teasing him about Nat's invisible rats.

The smile curving his own lips in response stayed firm all the way out of the hatch and back to the captain's cabin.

He knocked twice and entered only after the captain told him, "Come."

"Nathaniel? Does Mister Trupt have a message for me? I wasn't expecting you back, was I?"

The device lay in shambles across the offending charts, gears and rods scattered around the main base.

Nat crossed to the table, sorting the gears into groups in his head, marking them with knowledge gained in the shipyard and below.

"Nathaniel?"

Nat pulled his gaze from the pieces. "I thought about what you said, about this device being our only hope, and wondered if you'd like a hand. I've learned a bit about mechanical pieces in my time below decks."

He froze, half expecting a dismissal from the surprise on the professor's face.

"What an excellent idea, Nathaniel. I always knew you had it in you. Come, come, pull up a chair and let's get to work. It can't be that difficult."

Relief rushed through him even as he doubted the captain's confidence. At least he could do something more than sit out on the deck with the rest, contemplating how long before even their short rations would dwindle.

21

Sam wiped her sweating brow with one sleeve, her mind bringing up lectures from her sister about how a young lady should behave. She missed Lily, she missed Henry, and she missed her workshop where she didn't have to be afraid of what she was. As wet as her forehead became, her lips seemed drier in contrast. She fought the urge to lick them, having learned it only made them worse.

Nat had come with breakfast so long ago. He'd said then he'd return with water, or had she only imagined the words. At this point, Sam couldn't be sure of anything. Her head spun dreams with the heat, visions dancing on the wood grain. Sometimes Nat's face seemed to appear in the darkness, but just as often she saw Lily or even her beloved mechanical man, the same one she'd betrayed and left secured in her workshop so he couldn't follow her. She'd been so worried about her mechanicals revealing the truth about what she was that she'd failed to consider how she offered the greatest risk. Of course, she'd thought to have Lily with her.

A vision of her sister as she'd been that last day, so weak and ill, tore through Sam with such force, she stifled a cry.

Footsteps on the stairs made her jam her fist even harder against her lips. Her body trembled with the need to stay still before she realized the pad of flesh sounded much different than the slap of Mister Garth's boots. The engineer did not adopt the dress of the other sailors the way Nat had.

Sam remembered seeing the same when she'd wandered the docks, and when she'd snuck aboard. Only officers wore shoes at all times, officers and Mister Garth.

Another creak as he stepped down onto the floor brought Sam's wandering thoughts back to the present. She must have missed his call, too dazed by thirst to track one moment from the next. But he'd come to fix that.

She headed for the hatchway, her thirst too strong to wait for him to come to her. Nat always did what he promised, even when his promises cost him so much. She'd never been so grateful for his loyalty than right now. Delusion would be followed by loss of control, and they could be stranded forever on this sandbar if she transformed the ship. She needed water to regain control of her mind, and of her abilities.

"There you are, Mister Bowden. I've been searching the ship for you. Never would have guessed you'd come back down here in the heat."

Sam froze at the sound of a familiar, but unexpected voice.

She'd been seen. She should have waited. She should have listened for the call rather than thinking it had passed unheard. She should have—

"What in the blazes is this?"

Mister Garth ducked into the pipes to grab her arm and drag Sam forward through two rows, unmindful of how her thin limbs slammed against the hard metal.

She squealed, in pain, in surprise, in fear, but he didn't even flinch.

"A stowaway. I should have known that big house boy was up to no good. He works hard enough, but every moment is a lie. Rats indeed. Did he bring you aboard for his pleasure? Are you his doxy? He think he's above the same rules as apply to all of us?"

Sam stared up at him, driven mute by fear, though her parched tongue would likely balk at the attempt to form words in any case.

He shook her hard, the motion making her brain seem to rattle around in its bone enclosure, her dizziness only growing.

"Are you damaged? Speak up, girl. I'll have the truth out of you, I will."

Sam could not get out a single word, nor could she imagine any that would offer a measure of safety. She'd already lost that what with being discovered. Now all she could do was to keep Nat free of her.

"You think holding your tongue between your lips will change anything? Stowaways have no rights, girl. They're thieves, the worst kind. Especially now when supplies run low. You and Mister Bowden both. No better than the scrapper who steals bread from a baby's hand."

His tirade continued as he pulled her through the rest of the pipes toward the hatchway and the crew's judgment.

She had no choice but to scramble after him or be slammed into every pipe in the way. Her mind and limbs full with trying not to get more bruises, or risk hitting one of the pipes hard enough to knock it awry, something the engineer would never have chanced had he been in his right mind.

She'd seen him angry before, but never like this.

His hand on her arm burned with more heat even than the sweltering room, and a vein pulsed on his face as though a blood worm had squirmed its way beneath the man's flushed skin.

All this came to her in flashes, her mind too seized to comprehend what happened or to do anything in her own defense. Each impression sent her heart beating a little faster and her chest tightening until she struggled to breathe as she stumbled after the engineer, tethered to him by his grip.

22

N at and the captain had worked the morning through and well into the afternoon. He didn't remember when Jenson brought them food and water rations. He didn't remember consuming his share either. His mind spun with gears and rods, and plates and screws, but they'd managed to put the thing back together. All that remained was to test the device, a shaky proposition with only the poorly done charts to compare against, but better hope than either he or the captain had felt in the morning.

"You ready to give it a test, Mister Bowden?"

The professor's eyes seemed bright, but the deep lines cut next to them proved his chipper tone a mask. So much rode on their imperfect abilities. Nat couldn't lay claim to a smith's expertise, and certainly not that of a crafter capable of putting together such a delicate instrument in the first place.

He'd done his work in linking up the gears, in finding homes for each of the rods. He could do no more, and yet it had to work. Without it, they'd drift on an incomplete heading, with no hope of fresh water.

"Yes, sir. Yes, I am." He tried to project a confidence he didn't feel. He'd done his best, and knew his assistance had made a difference. Whether it made enough of one, they would have to discover.

"That's the spirit, Nathaniel. Your mother would be proud to see the young man you've become." He clapped Nat on the shoulder, turning the motion into a shove toward the door. "Let's take it out on deck and see just what this device can tell us."

Nat followed the captain out of the cabin, hope and doubt vying for control until he sent both running as he committed to fixing the device, if not this time, then the next. He couldn't let Samantha down any more than he could the captain and crew. However long it took, he'd make the device find them safe passage to friendly shores. They had no other options.

The captain strode for the bow, heedless of the sailor winding ropes, almost tripping over another sailor mending sail cloth, and only missing the one busy sharpening Jenson's knives because Nat grabbed his arm and shifted him out of harm's way. They reached the bow without further incident, giving Nat a welcome rush of relief.

"You hold it like so," Captain Paderwatch said, lifting the device so it made a straight line with the horizon. "Go ahead. I'm mindful of how much your hard work made a difference. You should be the first to test it."

Nat struggled to suppress a grin as he stepped forward to squint along the line formed by one of the plates they'd screwed back into place. He concentrated with all his might, seeking something that would reveal both their location and the nearest resupply. They had only a vague idea of what the device did in the first place, and who was to say it didn't take time to reveal its information.

A commotion rose behind him, but Nat ignored it in favor of squinting all the harder. Mister Trupt would have the situation well in hand. The captain entrusted Nat with this task and no other. The device had to reveal something of use even if he must will it to do so.

"Mister Bowden."

He jerked at the sound of his shouted name, recognizing the tone of Mister Garth at his worst. The device slipped in his hands and would have fallen if not for the captain's quick catch.

Nat turned, shoulders already tense against the next tongue lashing even though he couldn't think of a thing he'd done to deserve it.

Instead of the engineer's flushed features, Nat's gaze fell on Samantha's terrified face. He'd never seen her in full light before. Here she looked even paler, red hair a flag of fire around her wide eyes.

"You're going to have to do something about this, Captain," the engineer said. "Mister Bowden saw fit to bring himself a little treat. He's been hiding her in my engine room and feeding her off our supplies. Rats, indeed. There's a rat on the ship, but it doesn't have four feet."

Professor Paderwatch turned to Nat, his expression grave. "Is this true? Nathaniel, I expected better of you. You're no different than any other sailor on this ship. No special privileges, and no extra freedoms. Sneaking a woman aboard is a serious offense." He closed his eyes for a moment. "And I can't protect you from the consequences of your actions. What will I tell your mother?"

Nat's heart sank at how quick the captain was to believe the worst of him. "I did not bring her aboard."

If anything, the captain looked more disappointed. "A man takes responsibility for his actions, no matter what the cost. Only a coward denies them."

"I didn't. I swear I didn't." Nat glanced to Mister Trupt, all the sailors having gathered around to see what came of this. "The first time I thought it was rats. I discovered her later, and the only rations I've given her were my own." He turned to face the captain fully. "I couldn't let her starve. No one deserves that, and if you'd cast her off, where would she go? So I let her keep hiding. That's all I did. She's planning to leave at the first port we go to. It's just we haven't gone to any. Please. She hasn't stolen anything." He dismissed the memory of Mister Garth's meal. He'd already paid for that loss with his time in the brig.

"Please."

At first he thought the faint sound an echo of his own pleading, but the captain glanced toward Mister Garth's prisoner.

"Please. I can pay my passage." She stepped toward the captain, brought up short by Mister Garth's firm hold.

Nat wanted to protest. Samantha needed whatever money she had for surviving after she left the ship. But he swallowed the words. Better she lose some funds than they leave her on the bare strip of sand that stood for the nearest island, one that would vanish under the first storm or high tide.

"Young lady, you can't pay for a theft with stolen coin."

"She's not a thief."

"It's not stolen."

They spoke together, quick enough to provoke a laugh from the nearest sailor despite the tense situation.

"See, Captain. Even now, with his secret revealed, he defends her. You going to believe he didn't know the doxy was aboard from the start? Or are you going to see the truth before your eyes." Mister Garth shook Samantha hard enough that she cried out.

Nat moved forward. "She's not a doxy. She's from a good family."

"What constitutes a good family sure has fallen on bad times," Mister Garth scoffed. "Just look at her clothing."

Nat jammed trembling fists against his sides and glared at the engineer. "Yes, look at her clothing. You'll find it's fine woven, as fine as the strips you saw holding together the pipes. She's been helping. She helped keep the pipes from coming separate in the storm."

"So now she's doing your work for you as well? Doesn't make her any less of a stowaway doxy, nor you any better."

"She was in an accident. Captain, you remember the carriage that overturned on the docks the day we left. She was in it. She was tossed out."

"Are you claiming now she's damaged in the head?"

23

Nat and the engineer fought over her as though she were a toy. Listening to them, Sam felt torn apart at the seams.

The shouting battered her ears, but knowing Nat condemned himself with every word tore at her heart. She couldn't let this happen. She couldn't do anything to stop it.

Emotions overwhelmed her until she wanted to scream, to cry, to run to the edge and throw herself over if only to make it end.

She'd meant the edge of the ship, but a tingle first in her fingers and then spreading up her arms warned her she teetered on a very different cliff with gears and aether tangled below instead of salt water.

Sam fell to her knees and covered both ears, her arm free as the engineer forgot her presence to face off with Nat.

"Cannot change," she muttered under her breath. "Cannot change."

Lily's chant came to Sam too late to still the bout, not with the yelling above her and tendrils of aether reaching out for her from so close. Her whole body shook with the need, wiping out her surroundings and all awareness of her situation.

The chant twisted on her lips, her mind knowing the truth when her heart still hoped she could pretend to be nothing more than a befuddled girl caught up in circumstances beyond her control. That the sailors might accept.

A Natural had no hope among them.

But the words that fell from her tongue said only, "Can change, can change, can change," until she could hear nothing else and all other thoughts drifted away on the same wind that drew the aether toward her.

She breathed it in, caressed and cradled it in her thoughts, exploring this new mechanical, exploring its dreams in favor of her own. She had been made for this, designed by a trickster god who wanted to make a mockery of the human need for control, both hers and the crafters who first created mechanical contraptions capable of gathering aether and condensing it into the semblance of a soul.

Who was she to deny their sense of self? Sam had no more right to existence than they did, and perhaps no more soul. What she did have was a purpose, a purpose she'd denied too long, kept buried and trapped when the mechanicals were left wanting.

She would deny them no longer.

Sam surged up from the deck, barely aware of the sudden silence that fell around her. She saw only the aether-shrouded gadget before her, the fingers clasp around it a minor annoyance to be ignored until they tugged against her attempt to lay claim.

It didn't matter. The aether gave her strength her weak body wouldn't have had, just as it lent her the speed to enact change on the moving gears of the carriage.

Soon she had the gadget reduced to its component parts, a knife filched from one of the sailors making both a pry bar and a screwdriver. The loose fabric of her skirt kept the parts from sliding along the rocking deck as she built an image in her head of what the gadget wanted, limited as she was to only the pieces she could claim from the gadget itself and a pocket watch she'd found on the captain's person.

24

I t all happened so quickly. One minute the captain had the gadget and Mister Garth was shouting at Nat, then everyone fell silent as Samantha moved faster almost than he could see, snatching the navigation device along with the captain's watch and dismantling both as though they just came apart in her hands.

He stared at her like the rest as his secret, his friend, became so strange he had trouble believing his eyes.

Then something the captain had said drifted across his mind.

He figured out just what this meant only seconds before the first crewman did the same.

"A Natural! Throw it overboard."

The sailors surged forward, but Nat got in between them and Samantha, barring their path with his body. The impact of their movement almost knocked him to the ground.

"Get out of our way," Mister Garth growled.

Nat stared the engineer down, knowing Samantha cowered behind him with no hope of survival. "No. I won't let you toss a young girl overboard."

At least the sailors had stepped back for the moment, giving him breathing room. It wouldn't last though. He had to come up with a better reason than his own objections. Mister Garth, his trust broken a second time, wouldn't hesitate to toss him off the ship right along with her.

"Are you blind, man?" This from Hassan. "That's no girl. It's a Natural. We're lucky it hasn't dismantled the ship beneath us even as it did that gadget. Think with your head. We know you're a decent fellow, but that thing isn't worth your defending. It's more dangerous than a shark swarm."

Nat shook his head, unable to see Samantha as dangerous no matter what they said. They didn't know her like he did. "She's been living in the engine room this whole time," he told Hassan. "If she wanted to dismantle the ship, she's had many a chance since Dover. Instead, she helped me fix the pipes. Even before Mister Garth recognized the need, she'd shored up a few using the only material she had. She sacrificed her skirt for the ship. Is such the act of someone dangerous?"

Even Mister Garth looked confused at that.

There'd been no sign of her true nature. She certainly didn't fit any of the information he'd had about Naturals or he'd have recognized her from the start. And like the professor said back in his cabin just that morning: if Naturals could be controlled, they could be the biggest boon since steam.

Only there'd never been a Natural capable of such restraint.

He glanced at Samantha in time to see two of the sailors sneaking around one side to snatch her away from him. Nat shifted to block them, only too aware of how futile his efforts were.

Then his gaze took in Samantha.

Rather than the terrified girl he expected, Nat found an almost manic concentration on a face burning with fever flush that made her blue eyes glow as she fitted one gear after another back together, making who knew what from their only hope to get out of here.

Doubt slipped through his defenses.

He saw nothing of the Samantha he'd shared his meals with or who'd worked at his side through the storm, protecting all of them. This girl seemed more like a creature out of myth, not quite here and most likely up to no good. What would have happened if she'd turned into this down in the engine room?

The question burned him, knowing if something had happened it would have been on his head for not reporting her presence. He couldn't even pretend they'd scared her into dismantling the device to build some form of protection. If so, she'd never leave herself so defenseless.

Had he not blocked their path, the two nearest sailors could have picked her up and cast her overboard and he doubted even that would have broken her concentration, though she might react to the gears falling from her skirt.

"Wait!" His cry bought him a fraction longer to put the pieces together, much like how Samantha assembled whatever the gadget was to become.

But the sailors had used up all the patience they could muster and quickly started to move forward again, leaving Nat to do his thinking aloud in the hopes he'd find some way through this that kept them safe without costing Samantha her life.

"If she's a Natural, the fear is she'll dismantle the ship, right?"

The nearest sailors called out, "Aye," loud enough to make his ears ring.

"But she didn't. I thought she didn't touch anything down there, but it's not that simple. She did touch things. She fixed the pipes. Who's to say she didn't fix more?"

Mister Garth shoved Nat's left shoulder. "I'm to say. I worked hard to keep the engine running so smoothly, and I won't have some 'un'-natural creature take the credit any more than I'll let you do so, boy."

Nat didn't miss how Hassan gave him adult status but Mister Garth seemed determined to strip it away.

He straightened his back and looked beyond the engineer to the other sailors. "How many of you told me the engine had never worked so well? How many claimed a miracle when the same engine took us safely through a severe storm?" He turned to the engineer. "Mister Garth, can new parts, no matter how well made, have such an impact?"

He could tell from the look on the engineer's face the man wanted to claim they could, to deny any chance Samantha had been responsible for the smoothest running the engine had ever seen, but for all his bad moods and quick accusations, Mister Garth prided himself on adhering to the truth.

The engineer stepped back, avoiding a response, but in doing so, making the answer clear to everyone.

The sailors lost their coherence, milling about the deck without the purpose they'd shown only moments before, but still not willing to step beyond the situation and let a Natural go free. They needed something more than just a hint of possibility. They needed a push to decide for Samantha, but if her fixes to the engine wouldn't serve, Nat had no idea what to say. Even worse, if he kept pushing them to focus on the engine, how long before the sailors remembered just what they blamed for being stranded so far from a good port or even an island large enough for provisioning.

Nat tried to think of something, anything, he could use to delay the inevitable connection between Samantha and their current predicament.

Some small part of his mind held the answers, but the rest of him seemed determined to fail, too trapped in the situation to see beyond it.

He glanced at Samantha in a desperate hope for some clue as to where he could go for a solution.

Under his pained gaze, she turned the apparatus she'd created around, tilting it one way and then the next, her brow furrowed.

The apparatus seemed to comfort her no more than the original had eased Nat's tension. In an instant, she'd taken it to pieces again, a scatter of parts all that remained of the contraption she had built.

"She fixed the engine." The words started from his mouth almost faster than he could conceive of them, comprehension falling into place as piece after piece linked into a greater whole. "She didn't break it. She didn't tear it to pieces. She fixed it."

"And because of that, we're lost somewhere on the ocean without a good supply of water and the food running low."

Nat couldn't see which of the sailors had spoken, but it didn't matter. He and the captain had figured out the only answer, but they'd been unable to make it a reality. "She fixed the engine, Captain," he said, staring at the silent professor who'd stood behind him, neither helping nor preventing his defense of Samantha. "Who's to say she can't fix your gadget."

"What do we care?" Mister Garth ground out. "I say we toss her overboard now before she takes it into her mind to do some more fixing, and the engine turns into a pile of gears like that one she has now."

A grumble went through the gathered sailors, but Nat tuned them out in favor of staring at the captain, willing him to catch Nat's meaning much like he'd tried to will the navigational tool to work all of a sudden. "You said it yourself, Captain Paderwatch. With the charts unreliable, all we can go on is your gadget. We can't depend on it when it's broken. We have to have it working. You and I tried, but failed. Samantha may be our best hope of revitalizing the gadget and finding our way to the nearest viable port. Without her, we may be stranded out here until the water's all gone and the food as well."

Though he'd been speaking to the captain, he felt the shift in tension from the sailors on every side of him now.

Horrible, unspeakable, things happened when a crew lost all provisions. No one wanted to hear the risk spoken aloud. At the same time, no sailor could give up a chance, no matter how slim, to avoid that fate.

"Please, Captain. Let her try."

The captain would give the final say on the question. Even with the crew's gruff mockery, they weren't so foolish as to deny the chain of command. The captain's word set the rules.

"Please. For the sake of what you'd have to tell my mother if you survive and not I. Give her the chance."

Captain Paderwatch stood still, contemplating his request for so long Nat felt sure all would be lost. Whether he would be thrown over with her seemed likely the last question, and one he would lose whichever way. Either his life, or the respect of the crew and his own self-worth, lay in the balance.

"Yes, Mister Bowden. Your argument is sound. If she can fix it, we'll be able to navigate to the American coast and recover from these disastrous events."

Again the sailors grumbled, but some of the heat had slipped from their tone.

"But—" And the captain held up his hand. "You will have full responsibility for her. Whether she succeeds or fails is on your head, Mister Bowden. Do you understand?"

Nat turned to stare at Samantha, well on her way to creating another contraption of unknown purpose. Everything rested on his ability to guide her knack, to take this strange creature and transform her back into the Samantha he knew, then help her understand the purpose of a gadget even he didn't quite grasp, and make sure she brought it back to life the way she'd managed the engines.

He had no choice but to accept.

"I understand."

"Very well then. Mister Trupt, stand guard over the two of them if you please. I want no interference, but should she head for another portion of the ship, you will seize and confine her."

"Yes, Captain."

Nat swallowed at these additional instructions.

He'd tied his fate to an out-of-control Natural when even in the professor's journeys, no word had come of a Natural able to manage the same ability they depended on to save the ship and every one of them on it.

25

S am fought the aether, fought the bout, but her hands kept moving, kept putting the gears in place and winding the springs. She only succeeded in making a mess of things, neither stopping nor giving in.

Memory of the first time she'd had a true mechanical in her hands rose to the top of her mind. Her sister Lily had begged her to put it back the way it had been, not knowing the mechanical man came to Sam already transformed with no memory of what it had been when the first crafter finished working the metal.

Broken. All it had been when she discovered it was broken. Cruel to put it back in that wounded state. Though just a little girl, she'd known even then it would be wrong.

She couldn't do it. She couldn't restore what she'd dismantled before she regained control.

The aether wept, cried, screamed in denial. She'd be kinder to somehow pull the aether from the components and blow it away than to leave them bound in a tortured, broken state.

Sam shivered with reaction, her hands moving too quickly to see, always changing, always linking and unlinking the gears, but without direction, without focus. She'd thought a bout meant the aether took charge of her, never realizing she not only rode the wave of aether-driven demand but could guide it.

A gear slipped, the metal moving fast enough to slice her finger.

The components fell from her hands, pain startling her out of the aether cloud for long enough to bring the outside world back into existence as her blood dripped down to stain her tattered skirt.

"You have to fix it, Samantha. Focus. You have to do this for all of us. It's the only hope of getting out of here."

The words came through in that moment, a voice so familiar it drew her further into the real world, though she struggled to understand the meaning.

"I can't." Tears sprung to her eyes and dripped down her face, drying into salt trails under the hot sun. She tried to gather the words to explain how cruel it would be to restore the device only to have them drift away from her when her gaze dropped to the gears and they snagged her once again. The aether wrapped her up, but no image formed, no demand or desire left to guide her as though it too had burned through all energy, leaving only a need so loud she wanted to cover her ears and eyes, but nothing could block it out.

Hands touched her face, holding her firmly on both cheeks.

She blinked and stared into the eyes before her until all she could see were his pupils.

"You can do this, Samantha. You can make it just like it was. You can make it work again."

No one, not even Lily, had been able to pull her free of a bout, but Nat's voice kept talking, his eyes held her gaze, and Sam could feel the aether settling into familiar lines.

She wanted to tell him why she couldn't do what he asked, that the shape had gone, and she couldn't return something to a broken state. She wouldn't.

"You can make it work again."

How many times he repeated the sentence before she could understand his meaning, Sam didn't know, but at last she heard him. He was asking her to change it. Not different, but whether the aether had asked for that from the start she couldn't remember. But he had given her permission to expend the gathered aether in the right fashion. No longer fighting it. No longer trying to restrain herself.

A burden lifted from her shoulders, and confusion went with it.

Focus returned.

The echo of the gadget spoke to her from within the aether cloud. She could see how it would take the shape of the earth from the aether currents, something only another Natural could have done. The device pinpointed the desired location much like a compass but with a wider range of possibility. This one had been tuned to find land masses, land large enough to support water.

Sam pulled away from Nat, barely aware of his hands dropping free as she licked her lips in sudden awareness of her thirst. The aether wanted to be able to find water as much as Sam did, and she could make it able. She could fix it. Nat had given her permission. He'd discovered her truth and yet still he believed in her.

That belief wiped away the last of her hesitation.

She could fix this as she had the engine. She could make it back into the gadget, the same as before, only better. Before it had been broken, crying out for her help. Now it would be stronger, faster, smarter, and it could save them all. She could do this. She could do what no one else would be able to. And she would help them, save them, not cause a problem.

Despite her hunger, despite her thirst, energy flooded Sam. She drew aether from the air to add to the gadget's portion until the space around her crackled with power.

She'd been born for this. She'd waited her whole life to be recognized for what she could do, for how she could help. They wouldn't cast her overboard and they wouldn't lock her up. They would be happy to know her.

26

Her eyes glazed over, and Nat thought he'd failed as the Samantha he'd known disappeared again behind the wild stranger's face. So much hung in the balance, and his faith seemed too fragile to count on.

Then he noticed no frown line appeared between her eyebrows.

Instead, a gleeful smile stretched her lips as she snatched first one and then another component from its cloth bed, not even stopping to suck away the bead of blood on her cut finger.

His head spun as he watched her, willing her to make it happen. This had to work. She had to fix this as she must have fixed the engines.

Surely even hardened men like the sailors wouldn't be so foolish as to throw away their protection from storms, not if she could prove herself. And she could bring them speedy merchant runs that would offer more coin for everyone.

Whatever their beliefs about Naturals and the dangers from same, this they saw with their own eyes. A Natural engaged in aiding, not mindless destruction. A Natural under control, or at least some semblance of the same.

They didn't know her like he did, but they must realize she had all the opportunity in the world to harm the engine what with her spending so much time alone with the hatch closed so no one could see her.

If she had hurt anything, he'd have been the first to call her out. But she hadn't. She'd helped them. She'd been their miracle.

He gasped, only then aware he'd been holding his breath as he tried to follow the quick movement of her fingers, tried to anticipate what she'd reach for next.

Samantha hummed a tuneless string of notes as she worked. The metal changed, bent, mutated to her will, or so it would seem had he not caught sight of the sailor's knife she'd pilfered. He couldn't have used it so, but the metal seemed to soften under her touch as though it wanted to transform as much as she wanted to transform it. The process fascinated him, similar to the workings of the skilled craftsmen at the shipyard and at the same time so alien as to seem impossible.

Impossible or not, the gadget started to take form before his eyes. Its frame became recognizable, its shape the same as what he'd held in his own hands, or close enough to it. For just a heartbeat, he craved the knack, wished he could feel the nature of the metal the way she must, but reality soon crushed that desire. His very life, and her own, hung in the balance, resting on her alien skills as no one ever should have to, and on his ability to guide her.

Had she been a normal girl, he could have talked them out of casting her over. Nat felt sure of it. He had enough friends among the crew, and Jenson could testify, willingly or not, that the supplies were no lower than they should be. What business of theirs if he chose to short himself in the name of her survival.

But Samantha hadn't turned out to be a normal girl. Far from it.

No wonder her guardian saw fit to send her to a cloister. Nowhere out in the world would be safe for a Natural. One weak moment, and she'd be revealed just as she had been here. He doubted any other group would treat her differently, not with how far the Natural lore had spread. Maybe the people on one of those far islands Professor Paderwatch had visited remained ignorant of Naturals and their dangers, but he wouldn't stake Samantha's life on even that possibility.

A sigh came from the gathered sailors as though from one mouth, and Samantha transformed back into a scared girl.

The completed navigation gadget rested in lax hands on her skirt. Her head hung low on her neck, red hair masking her features, but exhaustion showed in the trembling of her shoulders. A gift or a curse, her ability seemed to drain all the vitality from her, leaving her as limp as the sails with the ship caught in a lull.

"Take it."

He almost didn't hear her whisper, so faint against the constant rustle of wind through the spars and the creak and groan of the ship. Nat slipped his hands around the gadget, finding no resistance even when he brushed against her fingers. He shifted to a surer grip before launching to his feet and crossing the short distance to the captain.

Nat would have sworn the whole crew held their breath this time, himself included. Captain Paderwatch examined the device thoroughly, tipping it one way and the next as though unnerved by the thought of putting his eye to the scope.

The tension grew until Nat wanted nothing more than to snatch it from the captain's hand and chance his own vision to Samantha's crafting. He bit his lip and waited for the pronouncement, reining himself in with enough effort to make sweat bead on his forehead, a fact he could blame on the heat of the day, but he knew better.

Finally, long past when Nat had expected his nerves to snap, the captain crossed to the bow and lifted the device to his cheek. If anything, the tension rose higher, passing beyond what Nat would have thought possible as the ache in his shoulders spread to the muscles in his arms, making him aware he'd fisted both hands with as much force as he could manage.

Captain Paderwatch seemed the only one unaffected as he scanned the horizon, pivoting to look in all directions.

The crew ducked to prevent blocking his view, but the captain did not appear aware of anything between him and the world beyond.

"Well!" the captain declared all of a sudden, making more than a few of the crew jump in surprise. A grin took over the captain's face, broader than any Nat had seen before, even in his mother's parlor.

"Does it work?" Nat slapped both hands over his mouth too late to keep his question in. Better to let the news come out more slowly. He still had no guarantee this would be their saving grace, nor that the crew would recognize Samantha's hand it in.

"Does it work?" Captain Paderwatch echoed. "Does it work? It works as well as I dreamed. No, better. She did it. She fixed the device, and with it we'll never be stranded without a direction again, not even with the sky gone black with storm and no stars in sight."

He grabbed Nat's shoulder and jerked him forward, seemingly oblivious to the gathering and what decision waited on his pronouncement. "Take a look, young Bowden. See for yourself. It reads the lines of the world. Where charts are drawn with human hands, this device reveals marks made by God Himself. No more guessing whether an island is large or deep enough to sustain water. We have only to look through and see its contours ourselves."

The description made no sense, as alien as Samantha's movements had been, until Nat put his eye to the telescope. Laid out before him, he saw the curvature of the earth, a good-sized island in the distance, and further still the shape of a continent, for nothing else could run so deep or long.

"Amazing," he whispered, his vision of a greater truth unimpeded by either ship or crew even when he turned.

"May I?"

Mister Trupt was the first to request, but soon each sailor had taken a turn, all except Mister Garth, who stood glowering to the side.

27

S am's exhaustion vanished as sailor after sailor tried the device and walked away with wonder on his face. Never before had her labors provoked such a reaction. Even when her work helped, she could read the fear in people's faces, the understanding of what she was. Here, though, she had given them something a sailor would desire above anything else, and she'd done so without harm.

She tucked the remains of the captain's watch into the folds of her skirt, embarrassed to admit she had done some damage after all, if in a worthy cause. The gadget required an inner spring. Whether this piece had fallen out at some point or had never been put into place, the navigation device could not function without the power held in a strip of metal wound so tightly it created energy out of potential alone.

The knife she left lying free on the deck, unsure which of the sailors had contributed the critical tool to her. They would sort out its ownership among themselves once they finished admiring the results of her work.

Nat came to her side, his eyes bright with wonder.

Sam took his outstretched hand, forgetting the pocket watch until its inner workings scattered across the boards. She flushed a dark red from the heat radiating off her cheeks. "I needed some pieces," she muttered.

Nat bent to examine the housing. "You chose well with Captain Paderwatch's timepiece. Of any on this ship, he'd understand the need. We had no hope of fixing his gadget if we couldn't recognize pieces were missing after spending all morning on it."

She relaxed at his words, though she heard the warning beneath them and sent a grateful prayer heavenward that she'd found a spring in the keeping of one who would understand why the watch had to be sacrificed.

"There's no way they can cast you off now," Nat told her after storing the watch housing and scraps in his pocket. "Everything will be all right. I promise you."

"How can everything be fine?" Mister Garth asked from right next to them, his voice loud and sharp enough to catch everyone's attention. "This creature has proved what she's capable of, sure enough. She's capable of transforming gadgets against the will of their owner."

Sam shrank into herself, recognizing the object in his hand before he held it aloft for all to see.

"You might say Captain Paderwatch allowed the Natural to change the gadget, though I saw it snatch the device from the captain with my own eyes, but did he offer his watch?"

His hand rose to reveal the captain's watch chain. Nat may have pocketed the case to tell the captain in private, but it had not been the only recognizable component.

Nat jumped to his feet. "Would you have been able to repair the navigation device with no tools or gears? It's a knack, not magic."

His defense had less of an effect than the captain patting down his pockets with a look of almost comical dismay.

Sam wished for a rock she could crawl under to hide, but nothing of that sort existed here, and the sailors would find her wherever she went unless she took on their punishment for them and cast herself off the ship as a whole.

"Mister Bowden might be able to control the Natural, but will he watch her every moment of every day, never sleeping? What will she do when he nods off? Will she dismantle the engine to make it better?"

Sam had never heard the engineer speak with such a compelling tone. She could tell from how the sailors shifted to face him his words had found their mark. Though she knew Nat would suffer anything in her defense, it mattered little when Sam herself could not deny the charge.

"Will she take apart our compass? We all know what a Natural is. We all know the damage one can do. Is one gadget to wonder over enough to sway you? A lucky transformation to our benefit? That says nothing of what she'll do when given the chance."

The sailors closed on her, nudging Nat aside as though he didn't matter. She could take the small hope with her that they'd place all the blame on her shoulders, leaving Nat free to become a captain someday as he desired.

All greater concerns vanished as the nearest men seized her arms and legs to hoist her above their heads. A shriek issued from her lips as ice filled her veins. They were going to toss her into the sea. She would sink like a stone only to be torn apart by the beasts that inhabited the water.

Sam found energy where she'd thought she had none, twisting and kicking in a futile effort to break free. Nothing else existed except the forest of hands grasping and pinching her.

"Stop!"

Sam froze at the command in that voice, and so did the sailors.

"Put that young lady down this very instant." The captain waded through the bodies to where four sailors stood petrified, Sam still aloft.

"Yes, sir," said the nearest.

She found herself lowered to the deck where she stood trembling.

"Are you all right?" the captain asked, his friendly face a sharp contrast to the commanding voice of a moment before.

Sam nodded, her tongue incapable of speech.

He turned in a slow circle, casting a much less kindly stare on the men surrounding them. "What's this nonsense about tossing her overboard? She fixed the engine so we could pass through a terrible storm with minimal damage, and now she's fixed the device that will save us where the charts have failed. She deserves your thanks, not this."

One of the men opened his mouth only to snap it shut when the captain raised a hand. "Even worthless stowaways that pilfer supplies get more consideration than this. You know as well as I do dropping her here is nothing short of a death sentence, a long, painful one. I thought better of you men."

The contrite looks that swept through the sailors seemed out of place on their wind-hardened faces, but Sam couldn't find it in her to laugh. Her arms and legs felt weak from what had almost happened. If not for the captain, nothing could have kept her from that fate.

Nat cut through the gathering to stand at her side, his fingers curling around hers and taking a firm hold. His presence offered little protection, but Sam found her spine straightening and some of the tremors leaving her limbs. She drew on his confidence to find strength where before she'd had none.

28

Nat wanted to relax when Mister Trupt stepped forward, but something in the first mate's expression reminded him of the decision to let the engine take the blame.

"Captain, the men are not at fault for their caution. Mister Garth spoke truly. We all know about Naturals. Right or not, the only way to protect everyone is to lock them away."

The unusual command the captain had demonstrated against a mob drained away in the face of Mister Trupt's words.

Nat wanted to scream at Captain Paderwatch to stand his ground, to prove to the men he had what it took to command them, but everyone on the ship knew the first mate held all but the title, the professor included.

Nat tightened his hold on Samantha's hand, unsure whether he sent her strength or borrowed from her own.

"She helped us, not once but twice, Mister Trupt. Is this how we treat those who offer aid?"

The captain's words held wisdom, but his tone had diminished to that of a petulant child faced with explaining why he'd tied a cow bell to the dog's tail while it slept.

Mister Trupt leaned in to offer the semblance of a private conversation though Nat had no doubt every one of the sailors would know each word as those closest conveyed them back.

"You're right, Captain. I know you are. But this isn't a simple person. You may see a young woman, or even just a ragamuffin, but the men, see, they look on that face and it's a demon. A Natural is the monster in the depths come to sink us."

Samantha paled beneath the pink the sun had painted on her light skin. "I'm not."

The first mate looked directly at her, something Nat wasn't sure any of the other sailors had done since learning her nature. "It matters less what you are as what they think of you."

The pieces clicked together into a roiling mess in Nat's gut. The first mate would make the same decision as before, protecting the ship and its captain in the only way Mister Trupt knew how. He'd let the sailors' superstitions win.

An honest part of Nat had to admit he'd never heard of a Natural like Samantha, able to restrain herself even in the slightest fashion, able to direct her ability for the good of them all. Where he might see superstition because of Samantha, they had good reason to see fact.

"What would you suggest, Mister Trupt?" The captain's question made Nat freeze, and from the tightening of Sam's grip, she'd done the same.

The first mate seemed at a loss for possibly the first time since Nat had come aboard.

Mister Trupt was a good man. No matter how much he needed to keep the ship running smoothly, Nat couldn't imagine he would cast Samantha to her death. And yet how many options did he have? Given the choice between the crew and a stowaway, the first mate would choose the crew.

"You're not seriously considering keeping this creature," Mister Garth said, barging into the conversation in such a manner as to remind Nat their privacy had been an illusion only.

"Who's to say what it'll do next. It could just as easily set the engine to a strength greater than the ship's boards could handle in the name of making it better. If it's running wild come next storm, we could end up on a short trip to the bottom while my engine propels the creature to distant lands."

The captain grabbed Mister Garth's arm with a return of his firmer demeanor. "A girl, not a creature. She, not it. We do not question a person's humanity, not on my ship. Do you understand me, Mister Garth?"

The engineer gave a short nod. "Yes, Captain, I understand you well. *She* is a danger to this ship and everyone on it. Do you catch my meaning?"

Mister Trupt stepped between them, forcing the two men apart. "We are well aware of the situation, Mister Garth. Please see to your duties. We'll soon have need of the engine thanks to this girl."

The engineer flushed, the message clear to him and all others of the sailors, who scattered to their tasks without further complaint.

"Shall we retire to my cabin?" Captain Paderwatch asked. "We can discuss this concern without further interruption."

Mister Trupt glanced around at the sailors, clearly torn between wanting to stay on deck and make sure the work was completed to his exacting standards, but then he grunted a reluctant agreement.

Nat tugged on his connection with Samantha, making sure she stayed within his sight. He flushed as memory of Mister Garth's accusations rose, but he wanted her close not for the ship's protection but because he could not trust the sailors to keep to the captain's command with no one on deck interested in upholding the direction.

29

Sam followed Nat into the captain's cabin, unsure of what would happen, but starting to hope. From what Nat had told her about Captain Paderwatch, he was no simple man, but one who had traveled far and thought about everything that crossed his path. She owed him for the help he'd offered up to this point, but she owed him something more.

She took two running steps toward the captain the moment they crossed the cabin threshold, but came to an awkward halt with one hand outstretched as Mister Trupt blocked her path. The trembling started again.

Nat moved up beside her. "She didn't mean to touch anything. Did you, Samantha? Tell him."

Sam could not stop shaking, the day's events crashing around her all of a sudden.

"Step back, Mister Trupt," the captain said, his voice stern. "You're frightening the girl. Come sit down, Miss…?"

He stared at her in expectation, but Sam's mind seized on the realization she couldn't give Henry's name nor her own. Either would lead back to Lily and cause the trouble her leaving was meant to avoid.

The captain smiled. "Samantha then. Don't worry, Miss Samantha. You are safe in here." He put his hands on her shoulders and guided her to a chair that was bolted to the floor.

When he pressed, she sat, the motion unfamiliar after so long in the engine room with only the floor for a resting place.

A heartbeat later she shot up to catch his arm before he could pull away, what she'd intended before Mister Trupt interfered. "I'm sorry, sir. I'm sorry for taking your watch without asking. I needed the parts, but I should have asked. Henry always says to ask."

"Henry?"

She sank back onto the chair and shook her head, lips firmly pressed together. Her gaze fixed on the small cut on her finger which had already formed a scab, unwilling to see the anger at her refusal.

The captain watched her for a tense moment then nodded. "I understand. From what I gather, this Henry has risked much in your protection. Only right you do the same. In your circumstances, I'd be slow to trust, too."

"Captain, you should listen to your own advice," Mister Trupt said, moving to the captain's side.

"She transforms mechanicals, Dennis." His glance to the first mate showed who he meant despite the lack of formality. "She's no danger to people, are you, Miss Samantha?"

Sam shook her head again, hard enough to make her neck ache. "No, sir. I'm not. I swear. And I didn't mean to cause harm. I just needed to…"

"See? You've got nothing to worry about, Mister Trupt. The only thing at risk here is my fountain pen."

If not for his laugh, Sam would have cringed. Instead, she managed a weak smile. He seemed everything Nat said and more.

"Now that's better. You've had a hard time of it, I'd wager, and with a knack like yours, I wouldn't be surprised to hear you've never been out on your own before. Too easy to get trapped as you did on our ship. Don't worry about the watch. I can replace it better than my life and the lives of my crew. Without your help, we'd have had to set sail blindly, hoping the next island marked on those unreliable charts had more than sand to slake our thirsts."

"Thank you," she murmured, unsure how to respond.

"She's a polite one too, Nathaniel. I can see why you sussed out her background so quickly." He paused, a frown creasing his forehead. "Though I can't say I'm happy about your decision to keep her hidden, especially since it's clear you didn't know her nature. You should have been able to trust me to do the right thing. I would have expected better of you."

Nat flushed scarlet at the chastisement, but said nothing in his defense as he stared fixedly at his bare toes.

Sam shrank in on herself, her own cheeks burning with the knowledge of what she'd cost him. To disappoint a man he spoke so highly of must hurt as much as losing the easy camaraderie he'd established with the crew. And he gained nothing for it, not even her company. She'd be gone as soon as they landed at a viable port. If she'd entertained the idea of staying hidden longer in the quiet times between his visits, she had no choice now.

"Captain, this is all very well, but the men are not going to stand for her wandering about, not knowing what she is. And Mister Garth surely won't let her back into whatever space she'd found to tuck herself in the engine room."

The captain turned to face Mister Trupt. "What would you have me do, Dennis? She's clearly had a sheltered upbringing, and with a good family at that from her language and manners. Would you have me lock her in the brig?"

"Professor, no!" Nat burst out even as the first mate nodded.

"I was being ironic," the captain said with a twist of his lips.

"I've been locked in the bilge room. It's dark. It smells. It's no place for her."

Nat stumbled over his words in his haste, but Sam saw the answer in the first mate's look even before the man put it to words.

"It's the only way, Captain. Mister Bowden, I understand your concern, but you heard the men. They'll expect no less, and if you don't make sure she's secured, they'll demand more."

"Couldn't she stay in here, Captain? Out of the way."

The captain started shaking his head before Nat finished. "Dennis is right. Who's to say what would happen if she roamed loose." He glanced to her in apology. "No offense, Miss Samantha, but it's for your safety as much as the ship's. If you were able to move about, whether you did or not, every problem, every time something didn't go as expected, and they'd lay the blame at your feet. I couldn't guarantee none of the men would take it into their minds to solve what they see as the source, nor can I spare a man to keep guard over you, even if I knew who to choose."

His cheeks reddened before he added, "And you did take the device apart before I agreed. Whether you have control some of the time or not, there's too much at stake to depend on your ability to stay out of trouble."

Nat moved between the captain and Sam, blocking her view. "I can't let you do this. She stayed right with the engine the whole voyage and never harmed it."

Mister Trupt's face darkened, but Sam pulled Nat out of the way before the first mate could speak. She crossed the small space to offer herself to the first mate. "You are right. I can't argue on any of the points, even if I wanted to. Not changing the engine more than I did was as much due to hunger as restraint. You are being more than fair. I'm the intruder here. Only—" She turned back to the captain, fumbling for the button holding her pocket closed. "Let me pay for the watch. And for my passage." Henry's coin clinked in her hand as she pulled a large portion free.

Nat cursed, the word something she would have been scolded for if Lily heard it from her lips, but neither of the older men reacted.

Captain Paderwatch glanced into her cupped palm and lifted two of the smaller coins. "That's enough to cover the watch. It was not an heirloom, simply a working piece. Too much happens on a voyage to chance something I couldn't bear to lose."

She raised her hand toward him. "Take the rest for my passage, and whatever provisions you'll spare me." Until she added the last, Sam hadn't considered whether they'd choose to feed her, or even let Nat continue to share his portions. Her hand shook, but she refused to pull it, or her words, back.

The captain closed her fingers around the money with a gentle but firm touch. "You'll need that coin wherever you end up, Miss Samantha, and I've too much of a conscience to charge you a fee to rest uncomfortably in a locked bilge room. You'll be fed the same as the crew, little enough to pay you for your work on both engine and navigation device, unexpected as it was. Put your coin away."

She stared at him for a moment, stunned, before accepting the directive and tucking Henry's money back into the purse, then sealing the pocket's button.

Captain Paderwatch clasped his hands together, the coins she'd given him already secured in a pocket. "There, that's settled. Do you need to collect anything from the engine room?"

Sam shook her head, grateful she'd come with nothing more than the clothes on her back and with no need of the boots still there. After Mister Garth's condemnation of her, she'd do anything to steer clear of the engineer. She had little doubt he'd toss her overboard himself if given the chance.

"We'll have to see about that, then. Mister Bowden, collect a blanket and a lamp from the stores." He turned back to face Sam. "Lamp oil is scarce, as you might imagine, but if you're going to be locked up in that space, you should have light to eat by at least. I'll have the sailor who brings your meal light the lamp as well. Only don't let it burn too long."

"I won't. I understand. Thank you. I've gotten used to the dark."

The captain shook his head at her thanks, and Nat gave her a hurt look from the doorway, but Sam knew they'd chosen the best option of a list of poor ones.

The extra kindness of a blanket and light were just that—extra. From the captain's words, she understood this space would have no portholes, much like the engine room, but even less light would filter in. At the same time, it had the comfort of a blanket instead of shivering as she wrapped her tattered skirt around her.

"That's it then, Miss Samantha." The first mate's voice sounded gruff in comparison to the captain's cultured tones, but she knew from hearing Mister Trupt through the ceiling of the engine room that he used his softest tone. "Let's get you all tucked away now."

His touch on her arm was gentle, and she let him turn her toward the door. Nat might not want this for her, but she accepted the need and would fare well enough. At least the captain would see to it that she had regular meals and water so Nat could eat his full share. With luck, they'd reach a safe place to leave her soon.

The thought offered little joy, but she'd have to learn to accept it.

30

Nat returned from the storeroom with the supplies Captain Paderwatch had commanded for Samantha. His gut churned at the thought of her locked in that dark, stench-filled place, but she'd denied him the chance to stand up for her. The least he could do was make sure she'd be as comfortable as he could make her.

"Just where do you think you're going, Mister Bowden?"

Mister Trupt's call pulled him up short of the hatchway down to the bilge and Samantha's prison. He lifted the blanket. "I'm bringing what the captain told me to." Nat choked down the desire to call her their prisoner. He'd do little for his already shaky position if he antagonized the first mate, and he'd lose all opportunity to help Samantha.

The first mate frowned. "We're getting underway. You have duties to see to. Jones! Take these items down to the bilge room and get back up here."

"Yes, sir." The sailor wasted no time in sprinting over, grabbing Nat's load, and denying him the hope of seeing to Samantha.

Nat slumped as he made his way to the engine hatch. His best bet lay in working hard and keeping his head down. He'd lost so much, but at least Samantha wouldn't starve, and he no longer had to fear for what would happen should she be discovered.

The captain was a man of his word. She'd get the same provisions any of them would, and thanks to her repairs, those provisions should soon return to full size, maybe even with some fresh fruit to balance out the dried.

A firm hand closed on his shoulder and pivoted him around. "You're due up on the rigging, Mister Bowden," Mister Trupt said firmly. "The captain wants to be prepared for all eventualities. We don't know how much damage the engine sustained, and sail will be just as capable of getting us to fresh water should Mister Garth have difficulties."

"Yes, sir." Nat didn't argue, and in truth, he felt a little relieved not to have to face Mister Garth after all that had happened. But as he made his way up the ropes, he saw his new place in the order of the ship. He'd been denied Samantha's company and refused access to the engine room. Whatever privileges he'd come to expect were now lost to him. At least he'd been given a sailor's task. They could have pulled the raft from beneath his feet and sent him back to the professor's schoolroom after deciding his only value lay in keeping the captain out of everyone else's hair.

Nat tried to find pleasure in that grace.

He'd proved himself enough to be a real sailor, not just another gentleman's son cast out on the real world with nothing of value to offer. Somehow, the thought left bitter ash on his tongue. If he had to weigh Samantha's needs against his own position, he'd make the same choices again in a heartbeat, but that didn't stop him from wishing things had been different. If only he'd managed to keep her hidden long enough to find a safe port and see her off to shore without losing the regard of these men.

Hassan glanced the other direction when Nat reached his position on the ropes, and even Phil had found a different place to be. They would have drawn blood for him such a short time ago, staunch supporters even when the charge of theft hung over his head. Not now, though. He'd broken the unspoken rule. He'd endangered the ship and everyone on it, or so they thought. He'd made himself a pariah.

Nat wound his feet through the ropes, and the same with one arm, leaving enough movement so he could untie his portion of the sail should he be asked to. No matter what they thought or how they treated him, he had duties. He would not give them anything to question in his behavior or actions from now on. It could take a lifetime, but someday they might come to consider him one of them once again.

"'Ware," Mister Trupt bellowed from the deck. "Make fast."

All around him, the riggers secured their grips just as he had. Phil taught them well.

Nat watched for the gust of smoke from the engine chimney, running over the steps in his head. First Mister Garth would pump air over the coals until the fire burned hot. Then he'd watch for the bubbles in the boiler, and only then release the valve to send steam rushing toward the engine. And finally, once the engine's rhythm had grown smooth, he'd throw the lever to connect the paddles and send the ship forward on the heading Captain Paderwatch had determined the best hope for resupply.

This was what Nat loved about life at sea. The motions fell into patterns he could set a pocket watch by. Everyone had a purpose.

He frowned at the chimney.

Everyone but him. He'd had one purpose too many, and cast all of them aside.

Mister Garth could have used his help. The boiler sat some distance from the fire, while neither valve lay in easy reach. A weakness of design, perhaps, but more likely the expectation of two responsible for so important a part of the ship instead of one.

The engineer would have to rush about, checking for bubbles, testing the pipes for any weakness, making sure the fire stayed strong, and all of this while deciding when to throw the critical valve. No matter what stood between them now, Nat should have been down there to help him.

He hadn't realized he'd loosened his hold until just before the ship lurched forward with enough force to send several of the riggers dangling by a single knee. Nat missed that pleasure only because he'd recognized the change in the engine's pitch just in time.

The ship swayed and jerked its way in the right direction, smoke billowing from the chimney, and the decks groaning in misery as they strained against the uneven movement.

A steady stream of curses came from all around Nat, and he saw Mister Trupt striding for the engine hatch to find out what went wrong.

Nat didn't move.

He knew exactly what had happened. The timing with one man lacked the precision of two. Mister Garth had connected the paddles before the engine found its gait and the gear teeth their perfect alignment.

Nat shook his head, worried at the strain such an error had caused, but soon the ship found her balance, and the movement smoothed out just as it should have, paddles turning evenly, and the water churning out behind them into a clear wake.

There'd been a time went such a start had been common-place, only with the engine in worse condition, the effect had been less dramatic. Nat hoped none of the cargo had been damaged, or the sailors would be sure to lay that on his and Samantha's shoulders along with the rest. He didn't worry about Samantha. She knew the sounds of the engine most likely better than any of them and would have braced herself well.

He stared out across the water, wondering if after all he should ask the captain for a recommendation to move to another ship. While he had no trouble accepting blame for his actions, carrying every burden on this vessel for the rest of his career seemed an undeserved torment. His lips twisted in a wry smile. At least his presence would keep the men from mutiny and the captain's reputation in good order. As long as the sailors didn't cast him overboard to divest themselves of bad luck.

31

Sam pulled the blanket tighter around her and leaned against the wall farthest from the stench. The ship had been moving for some time now, though she had no way of telling how long in the darkness. She could still smell the lamp oil from her last meal, but without a flint, it offered nothing but a slightly cleaner scent.

The captain had been true to his word, sending a sailor in with a fuller bowl than she'd had to herself since leaving Henry's estate. It seemed ungrateful to wish for more, but she'd hoped to see Nat, to make sure he'd come through this disaster all right.

Instead, a stranger brought the meal, a man who gave grunts in response to her questions and refused to look her in the face even once her lamp shone bright. Still, she thanked him with all the graciousness her sister had trained into her. They had not, after all, thrown her into the ocean.

She drew both knees to her chest and stared into the inky black that surrounded her, fighting the sorry wish that Nat had been cast in here with her so at least she'd have some company.

This room stood as four bare walls except for the door, a chamber pot in one corner, and a wooden box provided to hold her meal and the lamp. Even had she been able to see, nothing here could hold her attention.

The ship had started off so roughly, she half hoped they'd let her out to check the engine. When it smoothed, though, she hadn't known whether to cheer or mourn. Damage out here without the parts to spare could condemn them all, but at least in the engine room, she'd had the engine itself to keep her company for all she'd cursed its demands. This prison sat too far to sense the engine, leaving her to wonder if Mister Garth's harsh treatment had left any weaknesses behind. She refused to think Nat could have been so careless, but memory of Mister Garth's scowl made her hope it had been Nat's error. The only other explain would be he'd lost his position because of her.

Sam closed her eyes, though it made no difference to her sight. Her fingers picked at the blanket until she worried it would fray as her skirt had done. She stilled them with more concentration than necessary. How she'd manage for however many days until they found a good landing, she didn't know, but manage she would. Especially now that the Continent lay a good distance from her, she'd have to find the control to live among others and keep her nature hidden. What better use of her time here than to practice that skill.

Maybe she'd be able to find a job in a pastry shop like Lily had worked in before Henry came to love her. Surely the Americas would have fewer mechanical devices to tempt her. She didn't imagine many of those wealthy enough to purchase such things had come to a rough new world. And yet, if the blacksmiths came, who's to say they wouldn't craft some for the challenge of it? Nothing good lay before her, but for her sister's sake she could never return back home and her current state had little to recommend it.

Her thoughts drifted.

Too awake to sleep but left with nothing else to pass the time, Sam imagined becoming a blacksmith's apprentice herself. Who could say whether she brought things into being with hammer and chisel or aether then? She could manage all manner of creations.

A faint chorus of agreement came through the wood behind her head.

Sam jerked to awareness, pulling away from the wall and backing until her feet bumped the chamber pot, though not hard enough to knock it over.

Mechanicals.

The wall seemed lined with mechanical devices just out of reach. They had not gathered quite enough aether to voice demands, but had enough for her to sense their presence and for them to respond to hers.

She trembled at this further proof the sailors had been right to cage her. Despite their nascent state, they'd clearly been drawn to her just as her first mechanical man had been on the streets of London. Whether she'd called to them in her loneliness or her mere existence was enough to give them the drive to seek her out, she'd disrupted the ship even without the intention.

Sam wanted to yell at them, to send the mechanicals rushing away even as she must have brought them to her, but if she drew any attention, Nat would suffer more than he already must have. Her best chance lay in ignoring them. Perhaps the sailors would come and gather the mechanicals up, thinking one or another of the crew had attempted to play a mean-spirited joke. After all, they knew even less than she did of how Naturals worked.

Should such a lucky event occur, though, the harder part would come in not calling them to her again, in keeping her waking mind focused on other things, and her dreams as well.

Sam gave a sour laugh at that.

She was locked in a foul-smelling room without a single window or fresh air. Her dreams she needn't concern herself with as they were sure to be nightmares.

Mechanicals never came to her nightmares. They were the stuff of dreams and fancy. She'd be left to suffer the torment of her sleeping hours alone, something she had reason to be grateful for if it would keep the devices in their place, at least until she left the ship for her new life, however harsh or long that might be. What the sailors might excuse once, they would not a second time.

32

N at stood outside the captain's cabin, feeling less confident than ever before and about to do something he'd
swore he would not. That he'd gained from his mother's
friendship with the captain could not be doubted, but he'd
never sought the benefit, never traded on their history for his
own selfish desires.

It had been three days since he'd seen Samantha, though,
and he had to know she was managing all right.

His hand trembled as he raised it to knock, but Nat took a
steadying breath and straightened his spine before rapping
firmly on the wooden surface.

"Come," Captain Paderwatch called out.

Nat closed his hand around the latch and pulled, committed as never before.

The captain glanced up from his desk where he was studying a log, or writing one, then turned back to his work. "Oh,
it's you, Nathaniel. I was expecting Mister Trupt. Have you
come to resume your lessons? You've been neglecting them
for some time now."

The captain seemed willing to let the past go and pretend it
never happened, but as much as Nat appreciated the effort, he
could not accept it. He could not pretend Samantha didn't exist.

"That's not why I came, Captain." Nat stopped, unsure
how to approach the topic. He'd expected the captain to raise

it first and to use that to make his appeal. The absence left him a little lost.

The captain turned to face Nat fully, examining him from head to toe. "No, I don't suppose it is as much as I'd hoped to see a hint of the scholar in you. What is so important, then, that has you standing ramrod straight as though you'd crack if you relaxed even a fraction?"

Nat flushed, his attempt at appearing confident as shaky as his confidence in this matter. "I came to ask a favor."

Captain Paderwatch laughed. "Is it so hard to ask such of a family friend? You've certainly not presumed much on the relationship so far that I'd be soured." He sobered. "It better not be to return to the engine room though," the captain added in a stern voice. "That ship has sailed, my boy, and took your chances with it."

Nat could see the disappointment in the captain's features though Captain Paderwatch had not mentioned it since that terrible day. If anything, it made his resolve firmer. Samantha deserved better than for him to turn tail and run at the first scolding.

"No, sir. I understand Mister Garth's feelings on the matter. As much as I regret the falling out, I have accepted it."

The captain relaxed into his chair. "What then? It's little enough to do a good turn for a friend, even one too young and foolish to recognize what must be done."

Despite his efforts to appear calm, Nat found his hands twisting together and could do nothing to still his fingers. He stepped further into the cabin and wrapped his traitorous hands over the top of the room's second chair. "I've come on Samantha's behalf."

Captain Paderwatch pushed to his feet, the log falling unnoticed to the floor. "We've been over this, Nathaniel. Even the girl recognizes this as the only path. I don't like it any more than you do, but the safety of the ship comes first."

Nat held his ground with all his might and used the same effort to keep his voice calm and even. "I do not mean to argue for her freedom. Not that. But you didn't see her like I did. She was starving, confused...lost. She's lived a sheltered life. I didn't know why then, but I could see it in her. I couldn't turn her over to the crew's justice, Captain. She didn't deserve the state she'd fallen into, and announcing her presence would only have made it worse."

The captain nodded. "I can see you feel strongly about this, Nathaniel, but the rules exist for a reason. As does the chain of command. You should have trusted me with it."

Nat stared down at his clenched fingers. "I wanted to, sir. Truly I did, but how could I reveal her to you without the crew finding out? It wasn't like we could march her from there in disguise. We know everybody on this ship, all of us do. The best I could do was share my rations, no more, and help her survive until she could disembark, none the wiser."

The chair creaked as Captain Paderwatch sank back into it. "It's the last that condemns you, whatever your motives, Nathaniel. A crew is a motley assortment of men brought together by one thing: trust. The men have to be able to trust you to do your part to keep the ship and its crew seaworthy. I have to trust you to bring to me the matters that are for my judgment and my judgment alone. You've broken both those for this scrap of a girl. I hope she's worth the cost."

"She's a good person, Captain. She bore her situation without complaint, asking no more than I offered and trying to take less for concern that I wouldn't have enough to keep myself fit to serve. And when the storm threatened to tear the pipes apart, she'd already begun to shore them up with the only materials she had, the very clothing on her back. If you knew her like I do, you'd understand. I couldn't do anything differently, not and remain an honorable man. I made sure the ship wouldn't suffer, but that she wouldn't either."

The captain stared at him long and hard until Nat had to struggle not to squirm under the intensity of the gaze.

"That's the way of it then?" the captain said in a quiet, introspective tone, a slight smile twitching one corner of his lips. "You understand she's a Natural. She's not like other people, and never will be."

Nat gave a tight nod. "I know that now. I didn't then. You wouldn't have thought so yourself. She showed no sign, and whenever she fixed the engine, it was before I found her. In the time I've known Samantha, she's kept to her corner, coming out only when I told her it was safe, and even then she'd like as not wait for me to climb through the pipes to her. Even starving, she was too shy or afraid of being seen. Terrified. I couldn't chance making it worse. And you saw what happened when fear took over."

Captain Paderwatch shook his head. "I didn't mean that you knew already. No matter how enamored you might have become, had you known she posed a danger to the ship, you never would have kept her hidden. I know that, and the men will realize it soon enough. We trust in your character. I just wish you'd done the same with mine."

A flush burned Nat's face and all the way down his neck. He'd been so determined to protect Samantha that he'd never considered his actions in the other light. He'd betrayed his captain, Mister Garth, and the crew. No wonder they shied from looking him in the face.

"Enough. What's done is done, and no good will come from dwelling on it. We must move forward and past this."

The captain shot him a stern look. "I am ready to do so, at least as long as you have learned your lesson, Mister Bowden."

Nat recognized the official question even without the use of his title instead of his first name. "Of course. Yes, sir. I have. I sw—" He choked down the last word, provoking another smile on his captain's face.

"That's good, then. So what was this favor if not to set the Natural loose among us? I promise you she's receiving proper care despite her rude accommodations. I suspect both she and you are seeing more food for your belly, thanks in part to a better understanding of how long our current provisions must hold out before we can replenish them."

Nat circled the chair until he stood opposite the captain, only the desk separating them. "I never doubted you'd feed her, Captain, but I want—need—would like to see her myself. She has no other friend on this vessel, and everything must be even more overwhelming with not just her presence but the secret she kept from me revealed."

The captain leaned his chin on one hand. "You bear her no ill will for lying?"

Nat shrugged. "How could I? Had I known from the start, I'd have been just as likely to treat her as some monster the way the crew did. Like I've been told all Naturals are. It is enough of a burden to carry without every friendly face she meets turning away in horror and chasing her down."

"You're a good boy, Nat, despite your failings. And you see the good in others as easily. Be cautious. Not everyone holds to the same standards."

He didn't know how to respond to the statement, or just what the captain warned against if not questioning Samantha's intentions. He'd argued that point past good manners, and doing so again would not win him what he desired. "The favor?"

he asked instead, pretending not to understand the captain's meaning.

Captain Paderwatch raised his hands in a shrug. "Who am I to stand in the way of young love?"

Nat flushed all the harder, but didn't see fit to protest the root of his interest, not if it would make his favor come within reach.

"You've certainly paid the price for where you set your affection. You've upset the crew, damaged your relationship with Mister Garth beyond repair, and cost the ship and crew the benefit of a larger engine team, a loss we all saw the result of when we got underway after so long at anchor. But weighing all that, no benefit comes from keeping you apart now, and if, as you say, terror had a hand in her behavior, keeping her calm may be our best defense against her somehow remaking the brig into an escape vessel."

"Thank you, Captain." Nat reached out to shake the captain's hand, but it pulled out of reach.

"Not so fast, Mister Bowden. While I see the value in giving you this boon, there will be rules. You are to bring her nothing but food, and the door will be guarded the whole time you are within. If you do or say anything to disturb the balance we've set by penning her, all permission is revoked without appeal. Neither shall you neglect your duties, especially as it will cost me the time of two crewmen. Is that acceptable to you?"

Nat struggled to smother a grin at the thought of speaking with Samantha and seeing to her comfort. "Yes, sir. Very acceptable. Thank you for your consideration."

Again the captain's mouth twisted on one side. "Time's a wasting, Mister Bowden. I imagine you'd prefer to spend what few moments you have between duty and hammock with gentler company than my own."

"Yes, sir." Nat barely had the words out before he'd turned to open the door.

Instead, it swung wide without his touch to reveal the first mate.

"Ah, there you are, Mister Trupt," the captain said. "See to it Mister Bowden is given Miss Samantha's next meal along with his own, as I'm sure I heard the bell a bit ago. And set a guard outside the door."

Nat watched the first mate's expression closely and did not miss the surprise that softened when a guard was mentioned. Even Mister Trupt had his doubts where Samantha was concerned, but if the guard eased his worries, then Nat hoped it would do the same with the rest of the crew. And he prayed the captain had been correct that the crew would get over their hurt sooner rather than later. Even with Samantha's company restored, Nat had never felt so lonely as in these past few days.

33

S am looped her fingers over each other for the thousandth time as she tried not to listen to the quiet murmur of the devices. She'd gone to the far side of the room, where the bilge stench seemed stronger, but still she could hear them. Either her connection had grown in this dark space, or the devices fed off each other to draw in more aether and strengthen. She feared they'd grow enough to demand her help, and how could she pretend not to notice them then?

A rattle at the door provided an all too welcome distraction, even though she knew it meant a brief moment of human contact with a sailor who wouldn't meet her gaze or speak to her. The light helped more than the food, though. As she lost the edge of starvation, she could no longer count on her weakened state to maintain control and must exercise it on her own, a difficult task when she'd give anything for a companion, even a mechanical who could do nothing but dance.

Memory of the first mechanical she'd adopted from a captured Natural distracted her so the door swung wide before she could cover her eyes. The light bore into her skull, blinding her with pain.

"What have they done to you?"

Sam blinked the tears from her eyes and uncurled from her failed attempt to keep the light away as it followed her now, seared onto the backs of her eyelids. "Nat?"

A blurry shape knelt beside her. She would have thought him a dream if not for the worry on his expression as her eyes adjusted to the lantern.

"I'll put the food over here and light her lamp," came a gruff voice. "I'll be right outside."

Nat twisted to the side. "Thanks, Hassan. We can use this lamp for now, though, and I'll light hers when I leave. To save oil."

A grunt not much different than the only response she ever got came from the sailor. Sam had a feeling that was her fault as well.

The door closed, and Sam heard the key turn in the lock, as if he thought she'd knock Nat out and run.

Where would she have to go, anyway? Knowing what had happened on deck the other day, they probably feared she'd head for the engine and transform it into something monstrous. She'd be more likely to seek the other side of her wall.

Nat sat down on the floor and pulled her into his arms, blanket and all. "Are you hurt? Have they been beating you?"

Sam jerked away from the comforting touch so quickly she smashed her skull into his chin. How he managed not to cry out, she couldn't imagine. "I'm sorry. I didn't mean to hurt you. I'm sorry," she babbled as she tried to rub his face.

Nat caught her hands tight and held them until she calmed down. "It's all right. You can tell me. The captain will not countenance such behavior."

"Why would you think such a thing? They've been a little gruff, and I'm lonely, but I have food and a blanket, which is more than I had when I snuck aboard."

He reached out and gently wiped her cheeks. "You're crying. And the way you recoiled…"

Sam laughed and threw her arms around him in a hug. She couldn't help herself. "Nat, no one has harmed me. No one. Your light caught me off-guard. It made my eyes burn and tear. The sailors, they knock in warning. They treat me all right, especially since they're afraid of me."

He returned the hug for a moment before they backed away, Sam turning her face out of the light so he couldn't see her blush. She'd been too forward, her delight in his company getting the best of her.

"Well," Nat said, his voice brisk. "That's good then. I was worried."

Sam twisted back and put out a hand to stop him. "You're not leaving?"

He jerked his chin toward the box Sam used for a table. "And have you eat your portion and mine as well? I'm not that generous."

Sam laughed with him, hiding her relief at seeing not one but two bowls. "You were generous enough when it counted," she said softly as she crossed to the table. It brought her too close to the devices behind the wall, but she focused on Nat, pretending their sub-vocal chatter came from sailors talking in their sleep.

He sank to the floor across from her and leaned over his bowl, inhaling deeply. "The meal smells much better than this place, though with a light it's not too uninviting."

She put her bread down and looked at him. "It's the company that makes the difference." Then she snatched up the bread and dug a big mouthful of stew from the bowl to hide behind.

When she glanced up again, he sat looking at her, his meal untouched. "I tried to do more for you, Samantha. I swear I did."

Sam reached for him with her free hand, glad she'd kept the collection of devices to herself. "I know you did. You did everything you could. I'm fine. I'm comfortable enough, and happier now with your company. I'll last in here until we reach port. It won't be that long before I'm able to leave the ship."

Nat pulled his hand free and stared into his bowl.

She wanted to tell him she'd miss him too, but that would only make it worse. Better he think she wanted to be gone from here and put this time behind her. She'd caused enough trouble on the ship, for him especially. She could not dwell on his feelings or her own. They'd all be better off when she departed.

A knock came at the door. "Mister Bowden, I have to get back to my duties. You about done in there?"

Sam started, having forgotten the sailor standing guard just outside. Usually they only brought her food and came to claim the bowls some time later. "You'd best be going, Nat. I don't want you in any more trouble because of me."

Nat stood even as he gulped down the last few bites of his meal. Her bowl lay empty, and he swept it up to join with his before picking up the lamp he'd brought with him and crossing to the door. "I'll be back. I have the captain's permission."

The key turned, a sign their conversation had held only the illusion of privacy.

Nat glanced at her with a smile before stepping outside, taking the light with him.

He'd forgotten to light her lamp.

His departure plunged her prison into more darkness than just an absence of vision. She had an unknown number of visits before she'd be cast out into a world of strangers once again, with little hope of a true friend among them.

Her conscience twinged at the thought. He might believe himself a true friend, but she was once again keeping secrets from him in not sharing her concerns about the devices.

For all she knew, the other side of this room was where they stored devices when not in use and her fears were groundless. If she asked, though, she just might put the same doubts into his mind as lingered in hers. She had so little time left with his company and didn't want to chance losing her only friend.

A thud above her head reminded Sam of the sailor who'd stood outside the door the whole time. She couldn't have told Nat her fears about the gathering of devices even had she wished to. He might have soothed her worries, but the man outside, the one who would not meet her gaze or speak with her for fear of something unnamable, that man would spread word through the whole of the ship, saying she endangered them even now, behind a locked door.

She'd seen enough to know the captain and his first mate would choose the crew over a stranger even if she weren't a Natural as well. She'd be tossed overboard with none but Nat speaking out in protest.

Sam carefully lowered the unlit lamp to the floor and took hold of the wood crate. She slowly dragged her makeshift table across to the other side where she now spent her time, and then returned for the lamp.

She couldn't afford the company those devices offered, and with Nat's visits to look forward to, she wouldn't need it. When she'd been just a child, she'd spent many of her days alone, waiting for nightfall until her sister returned from work. She'd survived that. She could last this.

N at accepted the bucket of salt water and a bristle brush without even a grumble despite the task rarely falling to him in the two years he'd been on the ship. Now that he could visit Samantha, how the crew wanted him assigned at some distance or how they quieted down when he came near didn't matter as much. He still hoped with every fiber of his being they'd soon remember all the good he'd done and forgive him, but their shunning no longer left him desperately lonely.

Two more meals with Samantha had passed, each time talking about unimportant things. He avoided any mention of his loss in status or Mister Garth, and she hadn't brought up her plan to disappear into the first port town they found either. Neither wanted to dwell on the harsh realities in what short time they had left.

The bristles scrubbed against worn boards with a hypnotic rustle, lulling him into a half daze. The sun pounded on the back of his neck, his knees ached from the hard surface, and his arm pushed back and forth. The sounds of the ship became a symphony, the creak of the masts a counterpoint to the calls from the men.

Nat belonged here.

And he knew Samantha did not.

They both had to gain their proper places, even though it meant never seeing each other again.

"Here looks like a good spot."

Nat glanced up with no real interest to find Phil settling in to repair some of the damage the sails had sustained. The rigger said nothing else as he began to work, but with the whole deck to choose from, he'd sat within reach of where Nat scrubbed.

Another sailor dragged over the fishing nets. They didn't run a fishing boat, but when supplies ran low or a lull kept the ship stationary, no one complained about some fresh fish to supplement the salt beef.

"Mind if I share in the supplies," a third sailor asked Phil as he settled in with some torn clothing.

Nat hid a relieved smile and kept his head down, not wanting to discourage what could only be an overture, the first step in restoring his place among the crew. It seemed the captain had been right, and his purgatory was coming to an end much faster than he would have thought possible.

"You ever hear about old Milner's ship?"

"The one that came back to the surface in a storm, unharmed though it'd sunk a year before?"

"No, the other one."

Now in addition to the other sounds of the ship, Nat had his favorite one, that of sailors exchanging stories, each grander than the last. He could learn more from their stories than ever he'd be able to experience on his own, after he filtered out what could only be exaggeration. Sometimes, though, he'd found the parts he'd been sure could not have been true had happened, and those seemingly commonplace ones existed nowhere but within the teller's head, added just to raise a story up one more notch and win points from his fellows.

"Never heard tell of an engine repair like ours though," Phil tossed into the mix.

Nat tensed. He wondered if he'd been wrong, and they'd chosen this space just to torment him.

"We'll have the best tale of all when this voyage is over. We'll none of us need to buy a pint for years to come." The net mender thrust his hook between two strands and tugged them apart.

The third sailor laughed. "They wouldn't believe a word of it. Nothing more unnatural than a Natural lending a hand, eh?"

Phil shifted the sail on his lap until it almost touched Nat's bucket.

Nat moved the salt water out of the way rather than break the flow of this conversation, needing to understand the underlying meaning.

Not a word of it held anger or fear. It seemed some of the sailors, at least, had decided to accept Samantha's work, perhaps even to adopt her.

"As if there's anything natural about Mister Garth making such changes," Phil cut in. "He's nothing more than a gnomish man with no talent for anything but raising his voice and banging a wrench on the pipes to clear a clog. How could we have thought him the one to make the engine better?"

Another sailor took up the cause. "Not even with the finest parts in the world could he have done so much. His abilities showed best in how badly the engine performed when we left that sand bar. I thought the pipes would burst, and there's men still working through cleaning up the spillage."

"He can't be blamed for that."

Nat flushed hot as he failed to keep back his outburst. He, of all people, had no business speaking of the engineer, whether good or bad.

The sailors turned to face him, making Nat squirm under their combined gaze.

"You'd be the one to know," Phil said after a long moment. "So tell us how Mister Garth did not fail to bring us smoothly up to speed."

Nat sat back on his heels, the brush still in one hand. "It's a two-person task. It was designed that way. We just never noticed the lurch before simply because the engine at full speed barely cut the water."

He waited for their reaction, knowing this to be a test. He couldn't tell, though, whether they'd expected him to rise to the engineer's defense or join in his slander.

The sailor mending a tear in an already worn shirt finished his work and bent to bite off the thread. Phil set another two stitches while the man with the nets moved to a new section. The silence beat down upon Nat, lasting an age though it couldn't have been even a candlemark.

"Well, that's it for me today," said the sailor with the shirt. He walked toward Nat, coming close enough to make Nat fight the need to flinch.

Instead of a kick, he got a clap on the shoulder. "It takes an honest man to stand up for one who cut the ropes out from under you. You are foolish, and stubborn, but a good boy all the same. And in the end, you didn't fight the necessary thing."

With that, the sailor continued on his way as though he hadn't given Nat the greatest gift he'd ever received. He hadn't been trying to win their favor in his defense of Mister Garth, and had expected to lose what little good will he'd managed to recover, but they took no offense. Even better, the sailor made it clear his willingness to serve, and to accept what Samantha had to suffer for the ship, had not gone unnoticed.

A tsking sound pulled his attention back to Phil, the man with the nets having wandered off.

"Mister Trupt will be none too happy with the job you're doing there, Mister Bowden. Best pay attention, or he'll have you do the whole thing another time, and you'll miss a chance at the top ropes. We could sure use your sharp eyesight. The captain says we're maybe a day out from the island where we'll be able to get fresh water, and maybe even fresh meat. Wouldn't want to miss that heading."

"That's for sure," Nat said, leaning his full weight into the brush. "Though I wonder whether deer are found down here on the other side of the world."

Phil stood and tossed the sail over his shoulder. "Only one way to tell, and that's to hunt them. I fancy joining up on the landing party myself. See if I can't bring back something with a bit of fat on it to flavor the meat. Salt beef gets old faster than it gets too dry to stomach."

Nat paused to watch the rigger stroll away, his cheeks aching with a grin he hadn't realized stretched his lips. Whatever prompted the change, whether his acceptance of the captain's rules for him to see Samantha or the island swiftly approaching on the wings of Samantha's modified engine, Nat would be the last to question or complain. He couldn't wait to tell her all about the sailors at the evening meal.

35

S am spent all too much of her time straining for the sound of the meal bells. She didn't hunger any longer, and could have done with less food truth be told, as she had little to do to burn energy in her prison room, but the meals now meant a visit with Nat. She'd stuff herself to bloated if it meant another moment with his company no matter how short. If nothing else, the anticipation helped block out the mechanicals against the back wall.

Her ears picked up a new sound, but not that of bells.

The hard soles of boots against wood came toward this space, one rarely visited except to bring her food and dump out the chamber pot, and those sailors went barefoot just as Nat did.

She pushed away from the wall, but did not come closer to the door, suddenly cautious. An unexpected visit could mean many things, few of them good.

The noise stopped, or she stopped caring, as the feeling she'd feared and craved all at once washed over her. Unlike the babble from the other devices, the one coming now had the pain of purpose denied, and enough aether gathered to push that pain on to her. It lacked the clarity such things usually had when they grew strong enough to catch her attention, but her sensitivity had grown instead.

Her hands pressed into the wood, a splinter sliding into her palm though she'd been unaware of moving. The other devices clamored for her now that she'd come within range, but their incoherent calls had little impact compared to the broken one. Even the pain in her hand failed to distract her.

If she could have, Sam would have torn her way through the wall to reach for it, talk to it, and get the answers from the aether. She'd take parts from anything nearby to stop its pain.

"I know you can feel it, Natural. These others might not have broken your control, but this one is like the navigation device you snatched from the captain's hand. I know a bit of what they say about your kind. It needs you."

The mocking, taunting voice was none other than Mister Garth.

The engineer had been bringing the devices. He'd done this, not some aspect of her talent she'd yet to experience in mechanicals beyond those devices she'd given new life.

"Why?" she whispered, unable to keep silent.

"Hah! I knew it. You might have the captain fooled, especially with Mister Bowden having his ear, but I know what you really are, creature. You are dangerous. You are a cannon ball waiting for the right spark to blow through the ship's hull and sink us all."

She bit her lip to keep silent, but the engineer wasn't done with his accusations.

"Any other sailor would have been tossed in there with you for what that boy did. Instead, he sits at the captain's table and has the run of the ship. He even gets to visit with his lady friend, bringing you who knows what. The guard at the door is a relief only for fools," he growled.

"A Natural of your skill could easily build something from scraps that would overpower even a full grown man. I've seen it myself, I have. If I thought for one moment the captain or Mister Trupt would listen to me, I'd have your cage searched.

But they leave me no choice. I'll make you show them your true nature before you have the chance to destroy anything more."

"Please, just take them away. I swear I have nothing." She pushed against the wall even as the words slipped out, desperate to help the device, and too well fed and well rested to have anything between her and a full bout but the wall separating them.

A bark came from the other side, less a laugh than a triumphant cry. "You pretend well, Natural. You look the part, and your soft voice can sway weaker men, especially those with only scruff on their cheeks to separate them from boys, but you'll get nothing from me. I know the truth. You have as much connection to this box as to any living, breathing man." He shook the device so something rattled around inside it, and the demand rose to a high-pitched whine in her head.

Sam clapped her hands over her ears, driving the splinter deeper into her palm, and sank to the base of the wall, too overwhelmed to move away.

She heard nothing more from the engineer, his last words daggers enough when she couldn't be sure whether he'd gone away and left the broken device to torment her, or if he stood there still talking, his words with less meaning than the aether tendrils demanding she do something to fix the device when she could not even reach it.

36

Every muscle in Nat's body ached, but the deck had never been scrubbed so well. Mister Trupt jokingly said he hoped it never would be again when he'd inspected the work, or the planking would be rubbed clean away.

Memory of the first mate's praise and the lack of serious undertones he'd grown used to ever since Samantha was discovered made Nat's smile grow. He knew Samantha would rejoice with him. She'd understand the significance of this turn of events just as he knew it would ease her burden because she blamed herself for his circumstances.

"Jenson, is the tray ready yet?"

"Have patience, Mister Bowden. The wait makes the heart grow fonder, or so I tell my lady loves in every port."

Nat laughed with the cook, but still stared at the pot where Jenson brewed tea.

All the water required boiling to make sure it wouldn't spread disease, but the captain had called down for tea leaves to celebrate the nearing island. The cook had a good hand with the brewing, but just this once Nat would have gladly suffered a weak cup for longer in Samantha's company rather than wait for a proper steeping. If not for the serving he collected for Hassan, who would be waiting outside the door, he'd have pressed Jenson further.

He'd already helped by cutting the loaves not just for the three of them, but for the rest of the crew, and even collected the bowls and ladled stew into them. Nat had nothing else to do but waste his precious moments with Samantha.

"Oh stop your shifting from foot to foot, Mister Bowden. You'll knock the boat off her rhythm." Jenson took a clean ladle and tested the color of the steeping tea.

"It looks nice and dark," Nat said from where he stood stock still, his feet firmly planted on the floor.

Jenson laughed. "Dark for the likes of you, I suppose, and it's never steeped long enough for where Hassan is from." He ladled out three mugs and placed them on the tray as well. "I don't want to hear any complaints, though."

Nat picked up the tray, already backing toward the door as he promised, "No complaints. Not a one."

The sound of the cook's chortle followed him out into the corridor. The whole ship seemed brighter, the crew's mood lightened by the prospect of a good hunt and fresh meat while reclining under shade, if they were so lucky. The air seemed to grow thicker with each day, chasing them around corners and below deck to spread heat along their skin where no breeze could offer any relief. But even that couldn't douse their pleasure at prospects much more welcoming than the slow starvation and thirst they'd faced a few short days before.

If not for balancing the teas, Nat would have raced the corridor and up the short steps. As it was, he called for Hassan as soon as his head lifted above the deck. "Hurry, now. Tea's getting cold."

"As if it's the tea that's got you rushing, Mister Bowden. It's love put the color in your cheeks. We understand better your doings now."

Nat ducked his head as a flush heated everything from his neck on up. "She's just a friend," he muttered, but Hassan heard anyway.

"Sure as I've been running the ropes since my hair touched only my shoulders, you've been bitten. In my country, it's nothing to be ashamed of."

Nat started for the bilge hatch with Hassan trailing behind. "In your country, the tea is bitter, so love must offer the sweet."

Hassan sped past him to lift the hatch. "And in yours tea's tepid, just like your love. Be the story, Mister Bowden. The one we will tell to every new shipmate for years to come."

Nat headed into the darkness while Hassan paused to light a lamp. "You mean the one to get you free drinks at every port."

The rigger's laughter filled the dark chamber where Samantha waited, a precursor to the news Nat had to give her and proof he didn't pretend in an effort to ease her worries. If anything, the crew seemed to have adopted his behavior as a grand love story now that they'd gotten over how he hid her.

Nat preferred the teasing to avoidance for all that it embarrassed him. If love made his actions more excusable than honor, he would not argue.

He paused outside the door to let Hassan turn the lock. Whether the crew had come up with their own way to be comfortable with what happened or not, no one offered to lift the restrictions on his visits, nor was he allowed to handle the key. Still, better this than spending his time wondering how she fared.

Hassan rapped twice to give warning, lifted his bowl and tea off the tray, and placed the flint where his meal had been since he kept the lantern they'd used to come down here to light his own meal. "I'll leave the door ajar long enough for you to light the lamp, but be quick about it. Your countryman's idea of tea tastes all the weaker when gone cold."

Nat waited for the door to swing wide, opening into the corridor to prevent anyone from hiding behind the solid wood. The splash of light showed him the crate Samantha used for a table, though she'd moved it to the other side from when he'd last visited. He didn't see her, but he knew she'd be waiting for her eyes to adjust once he lit the lamp, warned by Hassan's knock.

Samantha?"

The sound of her name brought with it vague awareness of light fighting the darkness of her prison. Then gentle hands drew her onto her feet and across to the table. It wasn't far enough. The strident demands of the broken device had changed to desperate pleas, but she still could do nothing.

"You're hurt. Let me see to that."

Nat's voice had brought her back from the edge of a bout before, and she grabbed hold of the knowledge he'd returned to her. That gave her the strength to push the device and its aether tendrils away until she could see his face and know him.

He bent over her hand, tugging it into the light so he could see better.

She didn't know what he was doing until he touched the edge of the splinter and she remembered a bite of pain forgotten in the mechanical's cries.

"That's in deep. This is going to hurt."

Before she could guess what he was about, Nat ducked down and pulled the splinter free with his teeth. He probed the hole, bringing tears to her eyes. "There. I got it all."

Sam relaxed just in time to be scalded with hot liquid. She yelped and jerked her hand free.

"Sorry," Nat said, a sentiment denied by his grin. "If I'd told you, you would have said no. It's a waste of good tea, but

I wouldn't want you to get an infection, especially not down here."

Sam cradled her hand, a part of her grateful for the sting. It helped quiet the aether's call for all that it wasn't comfortable. "You are too happy about this by far," she accused.

He pushed a mug and bowl toward her. Sam noticed this one had liquid almost to the brim, the sacrificed tea coming from his cup, not hers. "There's much to celebrate. The captain says we're only a day out from an island big enough to support fresh water. You should hear the crew. They're counting on rich hunting and fruit to balance out our supplies."

She lifted the mug gingerly and took a sip. What he saw as good news meant nothing to her. While the crew resupplied, she'd still be locked in darkness, her only relief a port that brought with it the loss of friendship.

"Don't you understand? This means you're not to blame. That there's hope and everything will be better."

Sam stared at him over the rim of her cup. "How does hunting mean that?" She kept the thoughts about her own state to herself.

The change in Nat's color was visible even in the flickering light from the lantern. "I meant to say the crew is talking to me again. I know it's been a weight on your shoulders, but now that weight's lifted. I haven't lost their good will for helping you. In some ways, I've gained it even more. They're looking forward to using our story for tavern tales."

He glanced away, staring at the floor as though something fascinated him.

"What is it? You don't want your story told?"

Nat shrugged. "They think it's a love story, that you and I are ill-met lovers. It sparks the romantic in every sea man."

Sam's turn came to stare at the floor. "I consider you my friend," she muttered, "And it's not like we have any chance at a future together. We'll be parting at the first port."

"I know. I told them, but they don't want to believe me. We're just friends." He paused. "Their tales won't cause you trouble, will they?"

Sam gave him a twisted smile. "If I can't keep myself hidden from tales, how will I manage at all? Let them have their drinks. No one will believe the truth."

"You know of tavern tales?"

"These walls are not as thick as you might think." Sam spoke without remembering how Nat spent time in this very cell, but he did not chastise her.

"They aren't, and who knows who listens from outside."

He glanced toward the door, but Sam's attention went to the other wall, the aether-driven demands suddenly overwhelming.

She couldn't tell Nat what Mister Garth had done. She couldn't before, having already driven a wedge between him and crew, but she had to keep her lips pressed together even more now with their regard finally restored.

"You needn't worry any more, Samantha. A friend sits watch at the door, and it's not like you have any secrets left to hide."

She forced herself not to look at the back wall, picking up her bread to scoop some stew. "Thank you for tending to my hand."

"It must have stopped burning."

Though he laughed, she missed the distraction offered by the pain, especially as thoughts of what called to her behind the wall came back with full force.

"Tell me what it's like to change things."

She sputtered, stew dripping down her chin. Sam wiped it clean with the bread to buy some time.

Nat waved his words away with one hand. "You don't have to. I'm just curious. I'm curious about a lot of things. The captain would say it'll take me far and put me in trouble when I get there."

He grinned, showing an affection for the captain she'd suspected before, but his belief in the man had proved true after all. Most would have tossed her overboard just as the sailors wanted without another thought.

"I'd love to have a knack like yours."

Sam gave her head a firm shake. "No you wouldn't. Not and have to live the way I have. Your curiosity might bring trouble, but my very existence does the same."

"Has it really been so bad? I know it's hard now, but your clothes are well made, your words show a good upbringing… You're nothing like what I thought a Natural would be."

"I was lucky." She almost left that for her answer, but the urge to tell someone, to know that she had a friend who really understood what it meant to be her, proved too strong. The words tumbled out over each other, how her father had died and her sister had to hide her in an abandoned stable to make sure the police wouldn't find out about her. Then how she'd been discovered by none other than an officer, but one who laid claim to her sister's heart and held to principles that kept him from turning her in.

"Henry was wonderful. Is wonderful. He'd do anything for Lily, even make a home for me. Not that he disliked me, either. If you're my friend, he's like an older brother. I know he'll take good care of Lily with me gone." She stopped, the memory of her leaving sharp before her. Only with her gone would Lily devote her energy to getting stronger.

"It must have been hard for you to leave them behind," Nat said, pulling her back to the present.

Sam shrugged. "It was time to go. Henry needed to care for Lily without worrying about me. She'd never get better if she spent all her energy focused on how to keep me hidden."

"So they just cast you out? That doesn't sound very loving. You could have been captured, would have been if you hadn't found our ship."

His indignation made her laugh, a welcome relief from her concerns. "Henry found a place that was safe and good for people like me. He bought me passage and arranged the carriage to bring me there." She frowned, remembering Lily still thought her on the Continent. Somehow she'd have to send word.

"He sounds like a good man. Taking you and your sister both on when so many would have responded like the crew did."

Sam reached across to squeeze Nat's hand. "Like you took me on."

He looked away, but she could see the edge of a smile as he accepted the words.

"Could I beg a favor of you?" she said, speaking without thinking it through.

Nat spun back to face her. "Anything."

"You shouldn't be so easy with your promises."

He laughed. "You sound like Mister Trupt." A frown marred his face. "It's a pity you'll never have the chance to get to know him, or Hassan, or Phil. There are so many among the crew who would be as fascinated with you as I am. And they wouldn't do you wrong, not now that they've gotten over the shock and come to see your value, that is."

"I'll answer your questions. I'll tell you whatever you want to know if only you'll leave word for my sister when next you come to Dover."

Nat grinned and shook his head at the same time. "You don't have to pay me for the favor. I'd do it without. Not that I don't want to know about you, but I'll do better than that. Give me a note and his address, and I'll send it by ship mail at the next port."

Sam glanced around the room. "I would if I could."

"Oh, I didn't think. You probably can no more write your letters than the crew. Tell me what you want to say, and I'll scribe it."

She shook her head. "I can write a fine hand, Nat. But I have no pen or paper, and the crew would look poorly on you bringing me anything besides food, I'd guess. I can't cost you all you've gained."

"Oh." He fell silent, staring into the congealing remains of his stew for a long moment before he glanced up again. "I'll talk to the captain about allowing you this boon. It's little enough to ask, and the professor is not the type of man to leave a sister to worry about you when he could have a hand in preventing it."

Sam relaxed fully, relieved to have the strain of her sister's worry lifted.

Had she embarked on a ship headed for the Continent as had been intended, she would have arrived some time ago with word sent through Henry's contacts. Instead, they'd have heard nothing but that she'd vanished after the carriage toppled. At least Henry would know she wasn't captured, but the lack of evidence regarding her whereabouts would offer both peace and upset.

She started talking to distract herself from the knowledge that while she'd been at sea, her sister had been worrying even more instead of focusing on healing. Sam didn't really know what she talked about until Nat broke in with, "And how do you know what they want to be?"

Sam jerked at the question, realizing what she'd said only after it had already flowed from her mouth. She hoped Nat had been right about the sailor on the other side of that door. She'd given him much to think about in describing her abilities.

"Do you even know?" Nat persisted.

She'd given him the opening so could not condemn his wish to understand more fully. "I don't know, really. It's not like I have a map to follow. More like the aether forms the sense of it, and I work to bring the actual device and the sense to the same place."

"Do you understand what you do? When you look at a device, can you see how it goes together?"

Sam thought back to her encounters when just a child, limited as they were by Lily's attempts to keep her protected. "Sometimes I can in something very simple that cannot gather enough aether to demand. Mostly, though, it's like those devices behind the back wall. Even before they gain a self to ask, they whisper and mutter, but the broken one, it screams without stopping."

"What devices?"

Cursing inside her head, Sam focused on scraping the last of the bread crumbs from her bowl then pretended to drink the dregs of her tea, anything not to explain about Mister Garth.

Nat, though, had spoken the truth when he claimed the fault of curiosity. She said no other word, but she could see the questions spinning behind his eyes.

A moment later, he jumped to his feet, clearly deciding her lack of an answer meant ignorance he would have to solve. "I'll be back for the dishes."

38

Hassan had the door unlocked before Nat reached it, proof he'd been listening carefully. Nat waited for the door to close behind him before asking, "Do you know of any devices stored here?"

He kept his voice low, not wanting to worry Samantha. Nothing important should be kept here, especially not anything formed of metal because the bilge collected corrosive saltwater on a regular basis.

Hassan shook his head and picked up his lantern.

Together, they stalked around the brig to the far side where people rarely passed.

The rigger let out his breath in a long whistle.

Easily every device on the ship had gathered against the far wall in an orderly row.

"Did she do this?"

Hassan spoke quietly, but Nat imagined Samantha had sussed out what he was doing and stood against the wall next to them. He infused confidence in his tone as he said, "I know you heard as much as I did. It doesn't work that way."

His lips pursed as he contemplated the gathering. If not Samantha, then how did they come to be here? "Phil mentioned shifting cargo. Could these have been set here until the storage places are cleared?"

Hassan shook his head. "No one would be foolish enough to put anything here that couldn't withstand water. You know this as well as I do. Who would risk these? It must be her."

"Samantha wouldn't do this," Nat insisted, even as a part of him remembered how she'd said she just knew, how the devices told her what they wanted to be, but only when they'd gathered enough aether. Maybe the ship's devices had been too weak before.

The rigger clapped a hand on Nat's shoulder and gazed at him with sorrow in his eyes. "Love is a wonderful feeling, Mister Bowden, but it can make a man into a fool. You know it must be her. Think with your head, not your heart." He accompanied the words with a poke first to Nat's temples then his chest. "You know we'll have to tell the captain. The ship comes first. Go say your goodbyes. I'll wait for you by the stairs."

Nat recognized the trust Hassan gave him when the rigger handed over both the lantern and the keys to the brig, especially with all the ship's devices at hand. Who knew what Samantha could create from them?

She wouldn't though.

No matter how much the crew worried, Samantha wasn't like that. She'd told him how the broken device cried out for her help, yet she'd done nothing to get to it. She had control.

He lifted the lamp high, staring at the devices as though they could offer him a different answer than what Hassan had decided. If Samantha were here, she would tell him which was broken, which longed for a different purpose, and which had yet to develop a voice.

Nat shivered, the thought of gears and rods speaking too eerie to contemplate. No wonder most Naturals went insane.

He gave a bitter laugh at how knowing Samantha had changed him. Not so long ago, he had believed all Naturals were insane by nature, that containment was the only humane way to protect them, and society, from their uncontrollable urges. Yet, it still came down to this moment where a handful of devices could make all that learning meaningless by condemning Samantha with their presence.

The ship came first.

He could deny her actions as much as he wanted, but no other explanation presented itself for how they'd come to be here, undisturbed only because they lay against the far wall, a place rarely visited.

He lowered the lantern and trudged around to the door, not willing to test Hassan's patience more than he already had. Trust, he'd discovered several times this voyage, he could as easily lose as earn. His actions now would determine whether he was crew or traitor. He had no choice.

Nat wished he could go back a short time to the moment he'd seized on Samantha's words and hold his tongue.

Curse his curiosity.

Hassan might not have noticed the statement mixed as it was with so much else. Only after he drew attention to her comment about the gathered devices had the sailor come with him to seek them out.

They'd gone unnoticed for however long they'd been there, and might not have been needed until after he'd seen Samantha safely ashore. He'd done this. He'd condemned her to whatever fate the captain laid on her shoulders, all because he had to seek the strange behavior out.

His curiosity, though, still remained unsatisfied as if he missed something hidden within the discovery. Nat put his confusion into words, the mutter barely reaching his own ears much less the sailor who had already moved ahead. "If the devices could seek her out, why now when she can't fix them? They could have made their way into the engine room when she hid there, or at least gathered at the hatch, and had a better chance of reaching her. Even if they all hadn't grown capable, surely some would have."

"Hassan, wait!" Even before the answer fully formed, Nat ran toward the stairs and the sailor who prepared to condemn Samantha to the captain. "It can't be her."

Hassan stopped Nat's headlong charge with both hands. "With your head, Mister Bowden. You do yourself no good in this, and she is beyond the reach of even your fancy words."

Nat didn't fight the hold. He grabbed Hassan's arm and pulled him back toward the devices instead. "Look at them, Hassan. Look at where they are."

The sailor shrugged. "They hug the wall, trying to get to her."

Nat choked down his excitement to say only, "Why this wall?"

If Hassan couldn't see it without prompting, Nat's discovery could be dismissed as lovesick blindness just as his defense of Samantha had been.

"Why…" Hassan glanced from the row of devices back toward the hatchway, a frown wrinkling his forehead.

"You see it, don't you?" Nat asked unable to keep silent any longer. "If no one would store devices here, then they must have come from other parts of the ship."

Hassan nodded slowly. "And if so, they had to make their way down the hatch just as we did."

"Which would have put them on the first wall not the second."

Though Nat provided the answer, Hassan spoke much the same over him then slapped Nat on the back. "Sharp eyes, Mister Bowden. You're right. The only way she could have hidden the devices would be by her own efforts, and she's been under lock and key. This has a hand in it, but not one of hers. We need to see the captain still with a different culprit in mind. Gather the dishes and tell the miss goodbye. Hurry. This must be set to rights before the ship's put at risk."

Samantha stood at the door, the tray and dishes in her arms, with tears dripping down her face.

"Thank you for your faith in me," she whispered, stretching to place a chaste kiss on his cheek. "Even I had doubts, but you were steadfast."

Nat flushed as much from knowing he'd almost condemned her despite her belief as from the kiss.

"Hurry, Mister Bowden," Hassan said, giving him no time to confess his failure even if he could find the words.

"We'll get to the bottom of this, Samantha. I promise you."

He took the tray and kicked the door closed, Hassan turning the keys Nat had left dangling in the lock.

Nat hurried after Hassan, determined to make up for his weakness by finding the true culprit and seeing to his swift punishment.

39

Hassan, if it weren't for you, I'd think this another of Mister Bowden's misguided attempts to win favor for Miss Samantha."

The captain stared at Hassan and then Nat, who wanted to protest but knew this wasn't the time. He'd convinced Hassan to leave Samantha out of how they discovered the devices, saying it would only cloud the issue.

"I thought so too, Captain, Mister Trupt," Hassan said, shifting from foot to foot. "But if she'd brought the devices to her somehow, wouldn't they be at the nearest point, drawn like a nail to a magnet? She's never even seen the far side of the brig. It makes no sense for her to know space lay there enough for everything, and how would she get them to that spot without one of us noticing a device moving on its own. Not like she could choose a time when none were about. There's always someone."

Captain Paderwatch braced both hands on his desk and glared. "I don't need any more trouble, and that includes suspicions among my crew. We might be a day's journey from resupply, but the nearest port is some distance beyond that. If the men think one of them is trying to destroy the ship…" He shook his head.

"I understand the problem, Captain, but I swear—yes, Mister Trupt—I swear it's just as we described." Nat kept his voice even. "If you don't believe us, then come see for yourself."

The first mate rose to his feet. He'd been discussing the shore party with the captain when they knocked on the cabin door. "I rather think we shall, Mister Bowden. We need to assess the extent of this event, whoever is responsible, and it'll take more than one trip to replace the devices even with the four of us if your account has the least bit in common with reality."

The captain nodded his agreement and stood, waving for them to lead the way. "Until we learn more, I'd like to keep this quiet. There's been enough excitement on this voyage already. If it doesn't turn a tidy profit, I may lose some of the experienced crew to other ships."

Nat hadn't expected to return so quickly, but he knew from Samantha's descriptions that having the devices there must be a torment. He couldn't have removed them himself without raising questions that pointed to her once again, but the captain, and especially Mister Trupt, would not stand to have the devices in so vulnerable a position for long.

As they neared the stairs, Mister Trupt stretched his legs so he'd be the first to arrive. What he thought Nat and Hassan could have done if they got there before him, Nat didn't know, but at least this way there could be no question.

Silence fell as they clamored down to the bilge room, broken moments later with a whistle from the first mate like the one Hassan had given as light spilled over the collection of devices.

"They didn't exaggerate, Captain. Come see for yourself. Must be almost all of the devices we have aboard, from that potato slicing contraption Jenson refuses to touch to…is that the pump over there?"

Nat leaned past Mister Trupt to see where the first mate pointed, all too familiar with the shape of the pump after the work necessary to clear the engine room of water once the storm had passed.

Hassan pushed past Nat to collect the pump and bring it closer.

"Mister Trupt," Captain Paderwatch said. "This has gone beyond a simple prank. If the bilge had flooded, we'd have no way to pump it out except with buckets."

The captain sounded angrier than Nat had ever seen him, but he couldn't tell if the other men stared for that reason or because of the understanding Captain Paderwatch showed in his simple statement. The crew persisted in the belief the captain knew little of sailing or ships. As a learned man drawn to learning, Nat would have found ignorance more surprising, though the difference between understanding and experience still stood.

All thoughts washed from his mind as Hassan brought the pump fully into the light however. One side of it had been crushed, rendering the device worthless.

"This must be the broken one," he said, finally getting the answer to a question that had plagued him since Samantha spoke of the devices.

The three men turned to stare at him, Hassan with a frown and quick shake of his head from behind Mister Trupt.

"Look at it. It's been broken."

Captain Paderwatch gave Nat an expression familiar from when Nat had failed at one of his lessons. "That is not what you said, Mister Bowden, and you're not given to saying what you don't mean, especially when you don't mean to say it. Just what did you leave out?"

Experience told Nat he'd already lost this battle.

As much as he wanted to keep Samantha separate from this latest trouble, trying to hide her now would only make her look guiltier, and him the worst offender. "It's nothing important." He forced a shrug, trying to appear more at ease than he felt. "It's just that Samantha could feel them."

Mister Trupt straightened. "The Natural can feel the devices on the ship? And you didn't see fit to tell us this before now?"

Hassan moved forward to stand between them. "He just discovered it…as I did…when she told us of the devices. We wouldn't have found them otherwise, not tucked as they were around the side."

"Stand down, Mister Trupt. He's telling us nothing we didn't already know if we had given it a moment's thought. She knew I had a device on deck when she had no thought to taking in the scenery, not dragged by Mister Garth as she was. But that she can tell what's broken and what is not. Interesting."

"Yes, sir." Nat kept the pride from his voice, the deck already shifting beneath his feet. "She says they feel different."

Not for anything would he reveal she talked to them in her own fashion. A feeling the sailors would understand if they considered their own experiences, but which would make her seem more alien.

Half of sailing came from senses that couldn't be explained by any doctor's words. Talking seemed too much like giving the inanimate life, though, something sure to provoke unrest among even the most steady of the crew.

"Captain?"

"Yes, Mister Trupt?"

"We'll be hard pressed in a storm with the pump down, and if the engine falters, all the buckets aboard won't be enough to keep her afloat."

"Speak plainly, man. You say nothing we don't know already, but dwelling on it won't change the facts."

Mister Trupt ran a hand across his mustache. "She could." The words seemed wrenched from him.

"She could what?" Nat asked before the captain could get a word in. They weren't going to pin the blame for this on Samantha if he could help it.

The first mate gave Nat a half smile. "She could change the facts, couldn't she? She could fix it."

Whatever he'd expected from the first mate, after the man's reluctance toward Samantha, this stunned Nat. He turned to the pump, still in Hassan's arms. One side had been crushed as though hit repeatedly until it collapsed under the pressure. "I don't know, sir. It's seriously damaged. And I don't know what we might have for parts, either."

"Would she try?"

"I'd be happy to," came Samantha's voice through the wall.

Nat laughed though he knew it to be a serious occasion. "You heard her, Mister Trupt. She'd be happy to try."

The first mate's lips curled ever so slightly. "Then what's the harm in giving her a go. If she fails, we're still at risk in a storm, but we'd be no worse off."

"Unless she dismantles something else for parts," Hassan muttered. He shot Nat a contrite look, but it was too late.

Mister Trupt and the captain exchanged a glance before the first mate said, "Get the door open so she can get started, Hassan. I assume you didn't detour off to return the key as of yet. Mister Bowden, from this moment until the pump is fixed, you are relieved from all your duties except to give that girl anything she needs. The door is to remain locked when you're not present, and under no circumstances is she allowed to leave the room. Understood?"

He paused until Nat nodded, then continued, "Hassan, you're with us. We have devices to shift."

Hassan thrust the pump into Nat's arms, unlocked the door, and swung it wide. "Good luck," he murmured, though whether to Nat or Samantha wasn't clear. Nat had not missed how the first mate's command said nothing of failure in setting Nat's duties.

40

Sam met Nat at the door, fighting the urge to grab the pump from his hands. She followed close behind as he went to set it on the table, Hassan bringing a lantern in as well. She didn't need a light, though, not with the energy sparking the air.

"You know what they want of you?"

Aether already wrapped around her mind, Sam had to concentrate to hear his words. It took even more effort to frame a coherent response. "To fix it."

He caught her face between his hands as he had once before, leaving her to stare into his eyes. "The same as it was, Samantha. No changes. This is too important. And I am here to get you whatever you need. Just ask."

She forced her chin to nod, the aether demands like screams drowning him out, all but the emphasis on the last word.

He didn't need to tell her plainly. She understood this to be a test.

The first time, he'd turned a bout into a focused repair. This time she'd accepted the task as a craftsman might. If she proved her worth without the specter of lost control, the sailors would have less cause to fear her.

If the pump had wanted something other than to be restored, she didn't know if she would have been able to keep to that agreement, but it had a firm grasp of its purpose, a connection strengthened by the desperate hopes of sailors through every use over the years. She could feel the echo of those moments flowing through the aether itself.

He released Sam, as though recognizing he'd done what he could and the rest would be up to her.

She turned to the device and placed her palms against it much like Nat had caught hold of her. With her fingers, she felt the surface damage, but the aether told her where gears lay bent, rods crushed, and tubing torn open like a wound.

Aether painted a map to Nat's side, but Sam remembered his warning in time. "Your knife. I need it."

He pulled a sailor's knife from the sheath at his belt, no different than the one she'd stolen to fix the navigation device. From his half smile, she thought he remembered the same.

Knife in hand, everything else drifted away as she undid the fastenings and pried the casing free.

"Hammer," she ground out, fighting the suggestions of the aether in favor of the assistance she'd been offered. "Shilling gears, five, and a rod the length of my finger."

He passed out of her limited awareness though she retained enough to hear the lock turn. Presumably, he had gone to find what she'd asked for.

Sam bent to the task, using her fingers when she could, and the knife when she couldn't, to pry free the damaged gears, laying them out in a row. Some she could hammer back into shape. Others, Nat would have to get from their supplies, or maybe extract them from another device that served a lesser purpose.

Nat came back several times only to be sent forth again for more supplies. At first, giving directions to another person felt awkward, and she had to withdraw from the aether to figure out what to say. By the time she gave him the third list, though, his comings and goings became part of the web she wove to bring about the repair. Demands barked from her lips came with as much force as the device commanded her.

When he'd collected everything she needed, Sam set Nat to hammering out the housing. She did all the gears herself, knowing one bad strike could change a gear from recoverable to scrap metal, but the cover needed only to sit above the mechanism instead of collapsing into it.

His strokes, with their solid, rhythmic bangs, became a music underlying Sam's work as she shifted, sorted, and inserted the gears, rods, and pipe sections he'd brought her. What had been little more than scrap metal itself when it came to her now had regained its form and soon would regain its function too.

Sam reached for the last gear she needed only to have her fingers close on open air.

She sent a tendril of aether to find it where it must have fallen, but the space contained nothing of use.

The urge to dismantle the pieces and restore them into a different form swept over her as it had before when she'd lacked tools or components, but Sam pushed it down.

As though aware of her struggle, the banging fell silent. Nat had gotten as much of the original form back into the housing as possible with their rough tools.

"I need one last gear." The words came out with difficulty, exhaustion replacing elation as the bout eased even though she'd yet to complete the task. "It needs to be the width of my palm, no larger, no smaller. Can you find this for me?"

A strange look crossed Nat's face as he held up his own hand to measure against hers. "And with this piece it will be repaired?"

Sam nodded. "In form and function. It will be as it was before."

Where she'd expected relief, if anything Nat seemed to grow tenser.

"Can you get me the gear?"

His expression hardened, the Nat she'd befriended vanishing beneath a stern young man with a duty to complete. "I can."

He turned to go, leaving the door open behind him and Sam to stare after, wondering what would have to be sacrificed for this repair that caused him so much pain.

N at left the bilge area more slowly than on any other of his supply runs. The gear she needed existed in only one place—the engine room. He knew this because it had been one of the gears he'd help procure from the shipyard, and he'd seen it when Mister Garth had him check the spares for salt damage.

Mister Trupt told him to get Samantha anything she needed. He'd put no restrictions on that charge, the need for the pump superseding any other directive.

Still, as Nat approached the engine room, he dreaded confronting Mister Garth.

Bad enough that he planned to intrude on the engineer's territory. That he did so at Samantha's command could only make it worse. And yet, how else could he explain why he needed one of the few spare gears they had left after the initial repairs back in Dover and what damage the engine sustained during the storm.

"What do you think you're doing, boy?" Mister Garth said from behind Nat as he reached for the hatch. "You lost any chance of seeing the inside of my engine room again. Try now, and you'll be locked up beside your doxy. See if I don't make that happen. You're no better than a thief, and she's a monster. You belong together."

"Mister Bowden, what is your business with the engineer?" Mister Trupt appeared the moment trouble brewed as he always did though Nat couldn't have said the first mate had been anywhere nearby. "I thought you had something more important to do than go around stirring up trouble."

Nat fought the urge to slink away from that stern glance and straightened to his full height instead, a good hand taller than the engineer. "I mean no trouble and have no business with Mister Garth."

The first mate's eyebrows rose even as the engineer snorted.

"Why then do I find you with your hand on the hatchway that leads nowhere but the engine room?"

Nat looked from the first mate to the engineer and back, knowing his answer would not be well received by either party. It didn't help that he saw the captain approaching as well. With a sigh, he said, "I need a part out of the engine spares."

The engineer jerked toward him, stopped only by the first mate's swift intervention. "What right do you have to go rifling in the engine supplies?" Mister Garth sputtered, turning on Mister Trupt. "You heard the boy. His own words condemn him. He was off to filch some of my critical supplies. You can't let that slide."

"Let us take this conversation below," Captain Paderwatch said, moving past the three of them to lift the hatch.

The engineer balked. "I don't want that thief anywhere near my engine room."

"Mister Garth, need I remind you just who is captain aboard this vessel? It is *my* engine room, and I say Mister Bowden is welcome there if he has need of it."

Nat saw his own confusion mirrored on the engineer's face. He'd expected to win the argument when he made the need clear, but not for the captain to take his side explanation unheard.

Neither he nor Mister Garth made any comment as all four filed into the tight space below.

"I know your task is important, Mister Bowden, but if you could indulge me a moment, I think you deserve to hear this first hand," the captain said when Mister Trupt pulled the hatch closed once again, the clattering hum of the engine masking their conversation from any eager listeners.

Nat gave a reluctant nod, thinking more of Samantha waiting for him than whatever the captain had to say.

"Mister Trupt? Would you be so kind as to relate what you discovered in your investigation?"

Suddenly, all other thoughts vanished as Nat realized what this meant. "Mister Garth?"

The engineer wouldn't meet his gaze, but what of his face Nat could see in the uncertain light seemed flushed, as though the engineer knew what was coming.

"Well, Captain, as I told you, I asked about and it seems only one person has shown undue interest in things of a mechanical sort." The first mate turned his glare on Mister Garth.

"It seems, Mister Garth, your animosity toward Miss Samantha and Mister Bowden continues despite their respective punishments. What have you to say for yourself?"

"And it better be good," Mister Trupt interjected. "If we'd hit rough waters, you could have destroyed every one of those devices as well as the pump. Are you a fool? You'd sink just as quickly as the rest of us."

Any attempt at bluster drained with Mister Trupt's words, and the engineer's features became pinched. "I wasn't trying to harm anything. I was trying to protect the ship and the crew. You were too soft on the two of them. A Natural can't be trusted. You think they've been penned up all this time because of a misunderstanding? I don't know how she learned to hide herself among real people, but it's a mask. We saw it slip up on deck that day. The boy, he somehow turned her around so she ended up helping, but it could just as easily have gone very wrong. You believe the boy over me, but no one could deny the proof of their own eyes. If I could show you the truth, you'd cast the Natural overboard and she wouldn't be able to destroy us."

"You tortured her," Nat shouted, unable to contain himself a moment longer. "All she ever wanted was to help us, and you almost drove her insane."

"See," the engineer crowed, any deference forgotten. "He sees it too. If the boy's afraid for his lover's mind, we all should be."

Mister Trupt stepped between them, putting a hand to Nat's chest to restrain him. "You destroyed a crucial part of the ship to prove the Natural might do the same? If we had another brig, I'd toss you in it faster than you could snap your fingers, engine be damned."

"Wait. Hold on." Mister Garth backed away from the first mate. "I didn't destroy anything."

The captain caught Mister Garth by the shoulder before he could get very far. "Then just how did the pump, as necessary a tool as any on this ship, get so destroyed there may be no chance to fix it."

Nat chose not to reveal that Samantha had it all but working once more. The engineer didn't need to know.

"I swear I didn't harm it. I wouldn't. Not a crucial device like that, not anything on the ship. I'm no fool." He sucked in a lungful of air. "I'll admit I brought it to the Natural when she didn't react to the whole ones, but the damage, it came from the cargo shifts. You can ask Old Mick. I crossed paths with him on his way to deliver the bad news and offered to attempt a fix. He handed it over, and I snuck it down to the bilge, but that's all I did. If Old Mick thought I had a chance, it was wishful thinking. I doubt a blacksmith will be able to make anything but scrap from it."

"And you thought to accomplish exactly what by bringing it to Miss Samantha?" the captain asked, his tone deceptively mild.

"I know a fellow who works at one of the asylums. Where they confine the Naturals. He says they have to keep all mechanical devices as far from the inmates as possible. Naturals go mad when a device is within reach and will do anything to get to it."

The splinter in Samantha's hand flashed before Nat's memory. "So you were trying to drive her insane." His voice dropped to a growl on the last word, the difference between a deliberate act and an accidental one significant.

The engineer turned to look at Nat, and his expression held none of the expected anger. "Before she tore the ship apart in a storm? Sure I did. The ship and her crew come first. No matter how pretty that girl may seem, she's a danger to all of us, and you're no less of one the way you stand up for her. Why do you think you had to ask permission to go to her? Everyone knows you'll let her free given half a chance, and she'll take the boards out from beneath our feet."

"Enough!" The captain barked just the one word, and Nat froze in the act of fighting Mister Trupt for a chance at the engineer. He noticed Mister Garth froze as well.

"Whatever your intentions, Mister Garth, your misguided efforts put this ship and its crew at as much risk as ever Miss Samantha has done. I'll have to think on your punishment. Be thankful we have none here with the training to tend the engine or I might just have tossed you into the brig instead of the Natural you're so determined to condemn." He paused for a breath, but no one made any attempt to interrupt.

"You were lucky. No harm came to the devices or Miss Samantha, beyond what the cargo had already done. For now, you will help Mister Bowden obtain whatever he needs. That Natural you tried to drive out of her mind is busy helping once again. If she can save the pump, we'll have her to thank doubly should a storm strike before we reach land." He turned to Nat. "How are the repairs on the pump going, Mister Bowden? Any hope it'll work again?"

Nat took full satisfaction by watching the engineer's face as he reported, "She has it all but working. I found the parts she needed save one, and I know where it is. That's what I came to retrieve. One last gear from the supplies, and we'll have a pump come the next storm."

Captain Paderwatch relaxed enough to give Nat a small smile. "In your attempt to harm, Mister Garth, it seems you have done us a good turn. I would not have considered Miss Samantha a resource had you not put the device within her reach."

He sent the engineer a significant look. "Your trap was sprung, only you're the one with claws sunk into your ankles. See that you tend the engine and keep your head down. I'll have your meals brought to you. Keep out of my way. I have little wish to cross paths with you any time soon. Those who sow dissent among their crewmates rarely benefit from the results. You'd do well to remember that."

The captain headed for the stairs and up out of the engine room, but Nat was grateful to see Mister Trupt lingered. He didn't wait for the engineer, but strode to where the spare parts were stored.

In quick, efficient motions, Nat got the gear and returned to the stairs, happy to be out of Mister Garth's reach long before the first mate grew weary of keeping watch for him.

42

S am sat with her back pressed against the far wall, the same one she'd avoided when devices lined the other side. Her fingers twitched with the need to dive back in and do something to relieve the pump's craving for purpose.

Nat had been gone much longer than any other trip.

He'd seemed so confident. What if he couldn't get her what she needed this time?

She'd heard the warning in his voice. She had a chance to make things better, or to fail. He'd left no opening for the pump to become something different.

Bare feet thudded on the steps, giving warning in time to relax her posture so it looked as though she only took a break rather than placing herself out of temptation's path. Her expectant stare directed toward the still open door, though, most likely gave her away regardless of her attempt.

She could tell something had changed the moment Nat came through the doorway.

The tension had left his face.

That's all she noticed before her gaze brushed the gear in his hand and the aether that had been circling without anything to lay hold of fastened onto it with enough force to make her swallow a gasp.

"I told you I'd get one," Nat said, laying it on her open palm.

Sam managed to flash him a grin before racing to the table and inserting the final piece.

Aether latched onto the mechanism, coating it in a sense of purpose and success and dimming the demand that gave her instructions. Luckily, she could put on the housing with no assistance from the weird energy, and soon the repair was complete.

"And I said if you could, it would be fixed," Sam said, satisfaction lacing her voice where she'd all too often felt fear or frustration.

"It's done? Just like that?"

Sam tapped the housing which gave a somewhat muted thud back. "Just like that."

Nat stared at the mechanism, his head tipped to one side. "We should go test it, I suppose. Come on."

He swept up the pump, staggered as he adjusted to the weight, then grabbed Sam's arm as well, tugging her toward the door.

At the frame, she caught hold and broke free. "I can't."

A flush crept up the back of Nat's neck before it colored his face as well. "I'm sorry. I forgot."

Sam shook her head. "It doesn't matter. Tell me how the pump does, and I'll be happy."

Nat pulled the pump more firmly against his chest. "I'll be back before you know it."

Again she watched him leave, settling in for another long wait.

Sam imagined how it would be to live in a place where her abilities were celebrated, where she could have shown them her efforts and gotten cheers in response.

It took a heartbeat to realize the noise she heard came from outside of her dreaming.

Sam pulled further inside the cell, worried now at the door that still stood open. She could close it, but the key had left with Nat.

Feet thudded down the stairs then Nat reappeared, the pump no longer in his arms.

The grin stretching his face eased some of her tension, but she still pulled against his hold when he threatened to drag her out.

"Come on. The captain said it was fine. The crew wants to thank you."

His words broke her concentration long enough for Nat to pull her through the door, and when she reached the short flight of steps, hands came down and urged her the rest of the distance into a bright day. Or so she thought until her eyes adjusted and she realized it was overcast, even the billowing white sails failing to cast a shadow.

A cheer went up the moment she was placed on her own two feet, her daydream having come true.

Sam twisted, searching for Nat, who climbed out next. "What is this?"

Captain Paderwatch stepped to her side. "I should have known nothing remains quiet for long on a ship like this. Word of the broken pump had already spread, and with those clouds…"

He pointed to a dark line looming in the direction they now traveled. "Well, it seemed the lesser of two evils to reveal you had taken the pump in hand. A contraption like the navigation gadget is good for wonder and amazement, but most of these men would be more comfortable with a simple compass and sextant. The pump, though, that they understand."

His lips turned in a gentle smile. "To go into a storm without one means a hard night of bailing and a good chance of sinking. Seeing that once-crushed object suck out a bucket full of water faster than a blink…let's just say you're no longer a horrifying monster. No, Miss Samantha, it seems the crew has laid claim to you as fiercely as they have the ship. You are now 'their' Natural."

His meaning finally sunk in as Sam looked from face to face and saw only smiles, many on sailors she'd never seen before. Only one face seemed absent.

She could catch no sight of Mister Garth among those gathered.

Sam smiled wider than she could remember ever doing in her life, took hold of the tattered edges of her skirt and managed the best curtsy her sister had been able to drum into her. "Thank you, all of you. You have no idea what this means to me."

One of the sailors came forward, his knit cap twisted between his hands. "We're sorry, miss. We really are. You're nothing like we've been told of Naturals. You've helped us not just this time but three times over, and all we did was fear. Here. It's not much, but it's all I have to spare to keep you warm."

Instinct had Sam hold out her hands as he thrust the cap at her. She didn't know what to say.

That sailor was the first of many, both to apologize and to offer what little they could.

A small pile of goods collected around her, one sailor giving up his hammock, another a blanket as tattered as her skirt, but no less precious for that fact. Another had collected rags into a rough pillow. This he gave to her as well.

"Thank you," she said, time and again, but the gifts mattered less than the reason they gave. Where once she'd seen fear, if any would meet her gaze at all, now they welcomed her openly, if not as one of their own, than as a part of this ship. She'd never had that, never in her whole life.

Lily loved her, as had her father. Henry too, and some of Henry's staff, but every one of them, Nat included, had kept her hidden away, not willing to chance the reaction to her discovery.

Here, though, on this ship that Nat admitted was neither the newest nor as fast as most in the company fleet, the sailors had turned aside their fear to accept her.

Tears gathered in Sam's eyes, ones she brushed away and let the sharpening wind be her excuse. She'd never known as many people as this, and never had so many known her.

"Miss Samantha, I fear I have no other accommodations to offer you, but the wind's picking up, and I don't like the look of those clouds. I'd give you my cabin if we didn't have need of the charts, as poor as they are." Captain Paderwatch could not have looked more chagrined.

"I can stay right here," Sam told him. "I like the fresh air, and a little rain never hurt anyone."

He shook his head and waved several sailors over. "What's heading our way is no little rain. I'd have turned aside to avoid it if we didn't need the supplies placed firmly on the other side of that cloud bank. Thanks to you, we have the pump, and the engine's still going strong, but it's not likely to be gentle." He gave a crooked smile. "It would be a pity for you to be blown overboard now with your position finally settled, wouldn't it?"

"I'll take her in hand," Nat said, catching Sam's arm.

"See to it, Mister Bowden, and be quick about it. We'll be needing your efforts up on the masts to secure the sails."

Nat, Samantha, and two others brought her gifts down to the bilge room. The others stayed long enough to string the hammock before returning to the work of preparing the ship for a fierce storm. Nat lingered to make sure she was settled, but he had duties to see to as well.

As he crossed her doorstep, Nat turned back. "Wrap yourself in the blankets and stay out of the hammock for tonight. Only those accustomed to its sway can weather a storm in one, and even they might have trouble in a bad blow."

Samantha nodded, her eyes widening. "Will you be locking the door?"

The question startled him after all that had happened during the day. What kind of life had she lived that she'd think to ask?

He thought she might have brushed over some of it when telling him. She'd been far too willing to concede to the jailing before, and then to ask about it now as well.

"No. The lock was to keep you from destroying the ship. No one thinks you're out to do so any more."

"Not even Mister Garth?"

Again she surprised him. "You knew it was him?"

She nodded. "You didn't ask, and I didn't want to make trouble."

A quiet growl issued from his lips as he considered how she protected even the man who tried to drive her insane.

"He'll be punished, I promise you. But no one would stomach locking you up, even if I hadn't returned the key. Not with a storm coming anyway. The worst of offenders wouldn't be treated in such a way, much less the Natural who may have saved us all."

She had to be satisfied with that answer because he had no more time. He'd lingered too long as it was with the way the wind whistled through the spars.

"There you are, Mister Bowden. Get aloft."

Nat followed the path of Mister Trupt's gesture after closing the hatch. He scaled the ropes as quickly as he could without chancing his life, only taking one glance toward the engine room, already sealed against the storm. Mister Garth needed him down there, but he'd lost the right and didn't think the engineer would bend even with a storm bearing down. Nor would the first mate or the captain chance his presence serving as a distraction when they needed the engine to carry them to safety regardless of Mister Garth's fall from grace.

The thick sail cloth snapped and billowed in turns as the storm's fickle wind tried to dislodge the riggers working on securing the sails.

With the wind so strong, Nat knew Mister Trupt would have had them pull the cloth entirely if there were any chance of getting it safely below. Instead, he joined the others in wrapping the sails into as tight a bundle as could be managed and binding them with loops of rope pulled taut and tied off.

The dark horizon had seemed some distance when he went below, but in those few short candlemarks, the winds swept it right into their passage, stealing what was left of the day from the sky and turning the air itself into lashes against his exposed cheek. Nat worked with the others until every bit of sail had the best chance of surviving this violent blow as any of them.

Then the task was complete.

As though by a silent signal, all the riggers began their climb down the rigging in pairs, on the slim chance one could catch the other if he lost footing.

Phil became Nat's partner, and together they reached the deck first, risking a jump to the wood rather than attempt where the ropes became looser and chance a broken ankle if a leg got entangled. They crouched low, but stayed until the last of the riggers came free of the rigging, each making the same choice they had.

Together, the group scampered across the deck to huddle in the shelter of one of the shore boats.

"She's got a nasty temper," Phil shouted into Nat's ear.

He didn't bother trying to raise his voice above the thunderous wind and answered with a nod.

Hassan gestured toward the hatch leading to the crew quarters. It lay a short distance across the deck on a good day, but that stretch had little cover, and so came with a significant chance of being blown overboard.

Still, the storm could last a day or more, even with Mister Garth running the engine the whole time, or maybe more so because he had none to aid him in getting more coal for the fire or checking for breakage in the pipes.

They'd drown standing up if they stayed up top.

Nat reached for Hassan's hand, pointing from Hassan to Phil and so on until they formed a human rope. He could imagine Phil's comment about this being a rope even he wouldn't climb, or something of the sort, though the sailor made no more of an effort to open his mouth than any of them. Despite a deep thirst, this storm would offer them only salt water from how it had lashed the surface of the sea into a frenzy. And worse, the water would come with the force of the wake behind a ship with sails at full.

Nat made one end of their string and so set across the deck first, heading not for the hatch but for a point opposite them on the high side. If he timed it poorly, they'd be that much closer to the drink, but he'd watched the pitch enough to judge the high side would rise even more and cast them down to the hatch if only they could get out far enough.

As soon as he stepped past their shelter, the wind and rain pounded him flat.

He struggled to regain his footing and succeeded only when Hassan jerked him upright, the bigger man suffering less but still struggling.

They started to slide across the deck in the wrong direction. Nat's chest burned with the knowledge he'd misjudged and condemned them all.

A heartbeat later, though, the pitch changed, tossing them back to the other side, and over the hatch itself.

Nat reached for the handle, only to have his fingers close on air.

He had no time to consider the reason before not one hand but many caught hold of him and dragged each of the riggers, drenched and shivering, into the relative safety of the corridor.

"Move back. Move back."

Nat had already started lurching his way deeper before the call, but he attempted greater speed as sailor after sailor tumbled into the space where he'd been but a moment before.

Jenson met them at the other end with a small tot of rum, a fire for tea too dangerous with the waves so strong.

Phil and Hassan gave Nat's mug a light tap when they reached the pause at the bottom of a wave. "Good thinking, Mister Bowden. We didn't lose a one."

Nat raised his mug to acknowledge and almost spilled it down his shirt as the paddles bucked against the next rise.

Mister Trupt caught him from behind and steadied the mug. "I know you're new to it, Mister Bowden, but that's no way to drink your rum. Even that's not strong enough to soak in through your skin."

The others laughed, and Nat buried his nose in the mug, taking a warming gulp to hide his embarrassment even as the teasing warmed him more than the drink.

The storm they faced was as bad as any, the risk to the ship and crew high, and yet the sailors kept their humor. Some even seemed to be enjoying the wild ride up and down the hills and valleys of water. As much as he knew he should be terrified, Nat could find nothing in his heart but exhilaration.

"You're a natural seaman, Mister Bowden," Phil said before draining the last of his tot. "Ain't many of your background can take to the sea as well as you have."

"I'll take her any way I can have her," Nat shouted over the crash of a wave across the deck.

"Smooth and silky, or bad tempered and rough," the sailors all cried together in a call Nat first heard in a tavern at the docks. Some said sailors married the sea, and Nat understood why. He had a hard time imagining the return to life on shore, and he planned to do everything in his power not to have to.

44

At some point in the night, wrapped in both blankets and huddled in the far corner, Sam had managed to fall asleep. She didn't know how considering it felt as if every inch of her skin had bruises and she sat in a freezing puddle, but eventually exhaustion must have overtaken her. She hadn't noticed when the ship stopped bucking around her and settled back into a gentle sway. The motion had seemed alien at first but became so familiar she wondered whether she'd be able to stand on solid ground anymore.

"Samantha?"

She uncoiled her limbs and groaned at their stiffness. "I'm all right."

Apparently her response wasn't good enough for Nat as he appeared in the doorway a heartbeat later, then she saw he carried the very pump she'd repaired only moments before the storm hit with such force.

He raised it to make sure she'd seen. "We've pumped out the kitchen and crew quarters. The captain's cabin collected hardly any water and will dry. It's higher than the rest. I'm here to clear out your section."

Sam stood so she could wring the water from her skirt. "How is it working?"

Nat grinned. "As good as ever, though if it might seem a bit better, no one is mentioning that. The ship's riding low with all this water acting as extra ballast, so we're taking turns manning the pump to clear her out."

Rubbing a hand across her eyes didn't make the room any clearer, even with the door wide open and the hatch most likely as well. "Are we in the eye?" She'd learned that much listening to the sailors up on deck since she'd been locked in here.

"You think we'd be pumping out the water only to let more in? No, we steamed our way through it in the night. From what the captain says, we aren't very far off course either." He knelt to set up the pump, using her crate for a surface.

She'd bundled her lamp into the hammock with anything else she thought would get damaged. Though she knew they hadn't meant to be overheard, from what they'd said about damage to the line of devices, she rather suspected her room would be doused, though if they'd used the pump on all but the captain's chart room, little escaped the reach of such a storm.

Though distracted by her thoughts, Sam glanced back at the door, still puzzling over the absence of light. "Why is it so dark then?" she asked right out.

"Oh." Nat laughed, clearly matching her comment about the eye of the storm to this at last. "It's barely daybreak. You should take yourself up on deck. The sky after a storm is beautiful with a wash of color, and if you're lucky, you might even spy a rainbow."

"Can I?" The door had been unlocked, but even Nat said it was as much for safety as anything. Just because they welcomed the results of her labors didn't mean they wanted a Natural wandering about on her own.

"Go on. Another sailor's coming to help me with this. No need to wait. It'll be your first sky after a storm, an important step for a new sailor. You don't want to miss it."

He turned back to his duty, leaving the path to the door open and beckoning.

Sam didn't remind him she had no hope of becoming a sailor. Her journey would end soon enough, but that meant more than anything, she needed to collect what experiences she could before she left the ship with Nat, and its welcoming crew, behind.

She could barely remember the trip down to the brig, fear driving her more than curiosity and she'd been so stunned by the crew's response to her pump repair she hadn't bothered to look around. Now Sam took the time to glance at the space as she made her way to the patch of lighter sky that called her toward the hatch and the chance to explore.

At the top, though, she felt Nat's absence keenly and wanted more than anything to run back to his side.

Her knees felt weak and her fingers trembled as they held on to the railing, but she gathered her courage. Soon enough, she'd be on her own and unable to cower behind anyone. She'd helped these sailors, not just once, but twice now, three if she counted the engine. If ever she'd be safe and welcomed among them, it would be on this morning when each had taken a turn using her pump to lift water from their ship so it wouldn't sink them to the bottom of the seas.

As though to support her thoughts, the first rays of sunlight broke over the horizon, sending scattering lights as glittery as any of the jewels Henry gave her sister.

She didn't stifle her gasp of amazement, realizing too late how the sound would draw attention to her position.

"Well then, lassie," one of the sailors said, thrusting a thick-fingered hand at her through the hatch. "Don't linger down there or you'll miss the best of it. It's a gift for survival this light is. How you know you've made it through."

His rough palm scraped callouses with hers as he closed his fingers around Sam's hand, bristly hairs tickling her arm.

She lifted one foot to climb another step only to find herself flying through the air when the sailor gave a firm tug. Her shriek of surprise transformed into a delighted giggle, bringing back memories of Henry flying her about in circles over Lily's half-hearted protests.

The sailor dropped her slowly to the deck, keeping hold until she got her feet under her. A grin transformed the craggy face into that of a friend.

When he took a firm hold of her shoulders, Sam felt none of the tension she'd expected.

He turned her round to face the rising sun, and she gasped once more at the sheer glory of it, light turning the storm-tossed waters to precious metals, silver and gold in turn, with winking diamonds everywhere her gaze fell.

"It's the sailor's treasure, lassie," her new friend said. "All the wealth in the world out here. You maybe cannot hold onto it much past this moment, but it fills a heart, sure it does."

Sam breathed in the salt air, felt the sunlight touch her face, and understood his words not with her head but deep down inside, a part of her that cried out in recognition. Here she had found a place; here she would stay.

The pain the sensation brought into being made tears spring to her eyes. She turned away to hide them, but the sailor only nodded.

"It takes hold of a one that way, lassie. Don't you worry. None here will think less of you for feeling it."

Sam gave a gesture that was half nod, half a shake of her head, but before she could explain, Nat popped out of the bilge hatch as though springs were bound to his feet.

"Samantha, where are you?"

She brushed her eyes, blinked hard, then answered, "Over here."

Nat ran to her side, giving a grin to the sailor before casting his gaze over the waters as though drawn to them. "You watching over her, Seamus?"

The big sailor tugged his shaggy black forelock. "Aye, Mister Bowden. Keeping an eye on her, I was."

Sam turned to stare at the two of them, wondering just what place Nat held, or maybe what he'd done to make the bigger man back off, but a flash of color caught her eye instead. "Oh."

The two men stopped facing off to turn as well, captivated by the most magnificent rainbow Sam had ever seen.

"If ever there was a pot of gold at the end, this would be the rainbow," she whispered, more to herself than her small audience.

"That's only a tale, Samantha," Nat said even as the sailor gave a reverent "Aye" in answer.

Then, from somewhere above them, came the one sound even she knew to listen for, though she'd only heard the others talk of it.

"Land ho," the rigger called once more, and Sam squinted in an effort to see his pointed arm amid a tangle of ropes and sail cloth.

Beside her, Nat let out a whoop of laughter. "You were right after all, Samantha," he cried, pulling on her arm.

Sure enough, when Sam followed the direction Nat waved toward, there, at the end of the brilliant wash of colors where she'd expected the glowing curve to meet water, instead lay a bristling wash of greenery, enough growth to be clear even from this distance.

"Praises be," Seamus muttered, his fingers closing over a rough-carved Irish cross that hung around his neck. "It's land alright, Mister Bowden. And land with fresh water."

Before Sam could ask how he knew, more sailors joined them where they'd stepped to the rail for a better view.

"I'd guess fresh fruit hangs from some of those trees."

"And maybe even something big enough to hunt."

"A paradise for sure."

"A wild one from the look of it," said a latecomer.

Another punched him on the arm with a hard smack. "You thinking to complain?"

The soft-hearted bickering continued around her, but Sam only braced her chin on folded arms and stared at the land slowly coming clear. A wild land meant no port. No place to cast her lot among others. For now, at least, she'd found welcome among the crew, and with fresh meat and fruit in their bellies, they'd have no cause to complain.

The light danced along the waves still, a promise of riches no less compelling for its lack of substance. She'd take what this island haven had to offer her, and the future would have to wait. Insubstantial as it was, this land, this ship, and these people, would be her paradise.

Thank You for Reading

I hope you enjoyed the second book of The Steamship Chronicles. The series continues with the crew landing on the island, and just what Sam and Nat discover while there.

I love to hear about your experiences with my characters, so drop me a line in email to:

* author@margaretmcgaffeyfisk.com

or use the contact form on:

* margaretmcgaffeyfisk.com

And while you are there, if you sign up for my monthly newsletter, I'll share a bit of my writing and publishing journey, fun events, and even snippets or pre-publication stories as a thank you for letting me into your inbox. You can also choose to receive release announcements, which are split into genre and go out only when a new book is available in that genre. Feel free to select as many options as you'd like.

Finally, can I ask a favor? If you're willing, I'd appreciate an honest review of *Threats*. Your feedback will help The Steamship Chronicles find the right audience. If you choose to review on your website as well as retail and/or reader sites, you can also send me the link with permission to include it on that book's information page, if you're so inclined.

If you'd like to read an excerpt from *Gifts*, Book 3 of The Steamship Chronicles, please turn the page.

Excerpt

Gifts

Book Three of The Steamship Chronicles

The steamship's engine ground away, taking them ever closer to the island they'd spotted at the base of the rainbow. Every member of the crew seemed to be spinning fantasies about what they'd find there, though most of them focused on the end of short rations. The ship's progress felt all too slow when clear skies and calm seas kept the island visible but out of reach.

Samantha leaned against the rail and stared at the island with the rest of the off-duty crew. They'd probably been to many islands before, unlike her, but still, relief seemed only a small part of the excitement thrumming through them.

Perhaps they saw this as an adventure after all, especially after surviving yet another fierce storm. She couldn't be the only one looking forward to solid land beneath her feet.

"You'll regret the sleep you're missing come landing," Mister Trupt said as he swept by on his way to instruct some aspect of the ship. The first mate's voice held more laughter than warning, his understanding clear.

He came to a sudden halt next to Sam. "Thanks to you for your help, especially after…" His mustache twitched when words failed him, a state she suspected came rarely.

As much to ease his discomfort as her own at being put on the spot, Sam waved off the apology. "You did nothing more than what you had to."

"And I'd do it again."

He turned and left before she could determine whether his statement came as an acceptance of hers, or a warning of what had yet to come.

She might have fixed the damaged pump so they didn't ride too low after the storm, but her knack for repairing mechanical objects came from the aether they gathered about themselves, not any training or skill. Why should the first mate trust her to control the ability when even she wasn't sure she could?

The sour thought haunted Sam as the island neared.

The charts held no mention of this one, making the likelihood of a port slim. But once they'd resupplied, the captain knew the correct heading. Soon the sailors wouldn't have to worry about a Natural wandering their decks...or transforming what powered the ship from below them.

"And would you look at that," Seamus said at her side. "You've found us a beaut of an island, Miss Samantha. So much greenery means fresh water, and like as not some game as doesn't come already doused in salt, whether salted a purpose or tugged from the salty water."

He licked his lips in anticipation, and her thoughts strayed to a fresh meal all too quickly. She'd received the same cut rations as the others when she'd been discovered, and scavenged what she could as a stowaway before that.

A little hunger and short rations were much better than the crew's first reaction, though. They'd tried to toss her overboard on a sand spit that vanished and reappeared with the tides. A death sentence.

Still, she would do much for the taste of some fruit jam like Cook prepared back at Henry's estate.

Homesickness swept over her as deep as one of the waves crashing across the deck during the previous night. Her sister and Henry would be wondering why she hadn't sent word. If only she'd found Henry's man on the dock in Dover. Then she'd be safe in a haven for people like her on the Continent instead of half a world away surrounded by rough sailors.

"You're a wonder, Miss Samantha." Hassan changed his path to stop beside her after coming down from the rigging. "A king's treasure to be sure."

Her cheeks heated at the praise, and it washed away all thought of the English countryside where she'd hidden for half her life. "I didn't do much."

His wide mouth spread in a grin as he slapped both hands on the rail and laughed. "Not much? Not much, the miracle says." The other sailors nearby joined in his laughter. "You fixed the engine 'til she's strong, you fixed the captain's crazy navigation device so he can see the earth itself, you fixed the pump so we didn't drown…" With each statement checked off on his dark fingers, the sailors let out a cheer. Then his grin became wider still as he leaned close to whisper in the carrying voice every rigger learned, "And you didn't transform our ship into a top-heavy monster."

The laughter swelled around her, and Sam appreciated the sentiment more than they could ever know. She'd never been teased about her gift instead of feared before. Not even when she'd fixed the steam-powered heater on Henry's estate. Henry's people, most of them, had accepted her as Lily's sister despite her Natural tendencies, not because of them.

Still, she heard the warning beneath the joking statement. Not so long ago, they'd expected just what he'd described from her, and they weren't all that wrong.

No matter how much hunger and desperation had kept her knack under control in the many weeks of their journey, she'd heard the engine wanting more.

Sam turned back to stare at the approaching island as Hassan wandered off, having said his piece. He'd gotten his laugh and now returned to whatever duty he'd been about when he first saw her there. It wasn't as if he could miss her, the only female in a crew of hardened sailors. She was the youngest or next to it as well.

Thought of Nat sent her scanning the crew for her friend, defender, and companion.

He'd been with her the moment she'd seen the rainbow marking their path to the island, but he'd had other tasks to see to. No one had complained when Sam stayed up top to watch their approach, but then she had sailors all around her the whole time. If she were to do anything to make them nervous, she had no doubt they'd have her bound up faster than a sail with a storm coming in.

Oddly, the idea offered some comfort.

Here, she could trust them to stop her while still being kind. Discovery had always meant imprisonment in an asylum before. Despite the respect Henry's lineage, and his own labors, commanded, there would have been dire consequences for her sister and her brother-in-law as well. The ship ran on rules as strong as any on shore, with as swift punishments, but necessity and value weighed heavier than law.

And they found value in her.

HE CALL TO ASSEMBLE CLANGED from the bell shortly after they'd dropped anchor. It surprised no one and all of the crew had already gathered on deck.

Mister Trupt stood by the helm, the register in his hands. The list normally came out when it was time to divide up earnings, but even then it served tradition more than a true need. The first mate knew every name the sailors might have gone under, those of their own choosing and those given them.

Nat stood with the rest, no less eager to learn how he would be sent to the island. He wanted to discover whatever the lush jungle offered as much as any other despite his affection for the sea.

Mister Trupt called out the names, assigning some to hunting, others to chopping trees necessary for repairing the storm damage, and still more to seek fresh water to replenish their supplies.

Not once did Nat hear his own. Even when the first mate called out those allowed to take their leisure on the shore his name was not mentioned.

"The rest of you will be the skeleton crew. Keep the ship at ready. These are uncharted waters, and therefore hold unknown dangers, especially this close to land. Pirates or natives may pose a threat."

He snapped the register closed and turned to walk down to the captain's cabin where he would store the document.

Before he got free, the captain sprang up the short flight of steps with unexpected energy. "Mister Trupt, if you would, I need three of the men to accompany me on an exploration. This is uncharted as you've said. We will amend the charts and perhaps discover trade opportunities."

Mister Trupt scowled at the request, the ledger coming open once again as he considered his assignments.

Nat held his breath, sure this time he'd be loosed on the shore. After all, he had the most experience with Captain Paderwatch's research having kept the captain busy many a day when he'd first come aboard.

"Seamus, Pennybright, Hassan. You'll go with the captain after a visit to the armory."

Again the book snapped shut, the sound a bit more adamant the second time. Mister Trupt strode for the steps without allowing for any further interruptions.

Nat stared at the first mate, glanced at the captain, then returned his gaze to the one man with control over all shore access. Before he consciously started moving, his legs were already in motion, set on a path to intercept.

"Mister Trupt," Nat said when he'd come close enough not to shout. "Am I not to go ashore?"

The first mate's shoulders tensed. When he turned, his expression showed no significant emotion.

"Was your name called off the list?"

A flush heated his cheeks as Nat answered, "I did not hear it called."

"Then you're not to go ashore."

Mister Trupt spun and took the three strides necessary to reach the captain's cabin, but Nat could not leave well enough alone.

"But why?" he asked before rethinking the wisdom of a protest.

This time, the first mate's expression left no doubt as he glared down at Nat. "It could be because your actions have not been wholly trustworthy this voyage," Mister Trupt said, his words sharp. "It could be you sought to keep a stowaway hidden. It could be how you antagonized the engineer..."

With each statement, Nat shrank a little further, wishing his question unspoken.

"But the true reason is simple. You are responsible for Miss Samantha for all you've left her to her own devices this morning. She is to stay on board, which means so are you. Understood, Mister Bowden?"

Nat stared at the worn boards beneath his feet. "Understood."

"I did not hear you, Mister Bowden."

Nat glanced up, meeting the first mate's mild gaze firmly. "Understood, sir. I'll get on about it now, sir."

Mister Trupt relaxed both his stance and his face as he gave Nat a smile. "She's done much good and is sure to do more before we land somewhere civilized enough for her to depart. That weighs in your favor. But she is your responsibility, and fair or not, the girl has the ability to wrench the very ship from beneath us. She's not to leave your sight unless placed back in her room with the key turned. There will be no slipping on this, Mister Bowden. She will not be left to wander when so few remain aboard to monitor her."

Hearing the warning and knowing he'd been a bit too lax with the ship's rules, Nat could only nod his agreement.

"Wait here."

Mister Trupt left him to stew in his own shortcomings while the first mate entered the captain's cabin to replace the register. If not for the reputation Nat had earned since coming on board, first by keeping the captain from plaguing the crew and then by learning each part of the vessel with careful attention paid to those best skilled in the tasks, he'd have gotten more than a warning. He knew as much from when the engineer's false accusation almost ended with him hanging from the yardarm.

"Here you go, Mister Bowden. Take care not to lose this key, or our Natural. Mister Garth will be staying aboard to tend to some repairs. You are to keep out of his way and make sure Miss Samantha does the same. I will not hear of any trouble upon my return, now will I?"

Nat closed his fist around the key once used to lock him inside and now to keep the crew happy. Samantha ran free in the engine room for many weeks without causing any damage. It didn't seem fair to lock her up, especially after she'd repaired the engine and several other vital mechanical devices.

He sighed and thrust the key into his pocket. Mister Garth's story about the untrustworthy apprentice had shown well enough how expectations could be as dangerous as any reality even without his own experience with the crew's reactions.

A H, THERE YOU ARE, MISTER Bowden. I wouldn't have expected to find you already at my cabin door."

Nat turned to face the captain, half-tempted to renew his pleas to go to the island. He could bring Samantha with him, fulfilling both demands.

"Mister Trupt has much to do with preparing the equipment. We have sizable damage that I'm more comfortable patching here, with such a good supply of raw wood, than chancing a failure as we cross the wide stretch between us and the Americas. We'll be here for a number of days, I suspect, and so the crew will need a proper base on the island as well. Not to mention renewing our stores from what vegetation and meat we can find."

Captain Paderwatch got a dreamy look on his face that boded ill for Jenson. Like as not, the cook would be tasked with recreating something from the captain's extensive travels as a child and young man studying different cultures, something far apart from the simple fare the crew preferred.

"You wanted to see me?" Nat cut in before the captain got started into a tale of another voyage.

While Nat listened intently to the sailors' talk, the captain more often spoke of topics like food and marriage habits. It would be a long sail before Nat would have a use for such knowledge. Not until he succeeded in his effort to someday command a vessel himself.

The captain shook his head to clear it and narrowed his gaze to take in Nat rather than whatever he'd been contemplating from the past. "Right. Yes, Mister Bowden, I did. Step into my cabin for a moment."

Nat couldn't imagine what instruction the captain would consider so important as to delay his own explorations of the island, and the first mate had already given Nat a charge. If ever Samantha would get in trouble, this would be the time for it with the crew focused on preparations and no one paying any mind.

"Come along, Nat. I haven't much time."

"Mister Trupt—"

"Mister Trupt can wait."

Nat's shoulders curved as he gave in to the inevitable. He couldn't chance this being a true order, not when he'd stretched the captain's patience well beyond any friendship the man held for Nat's mother.

The door closed behind him with a finality that made Nat flinch. But then he'd been barred from the island. While the captain had better things to do, he must watch over Sam as the first mate commanded. He hoped she'd stay out of the way and take care.

"Mister Trupt put you in charge of Miss Samantha, did he not?"

The captain paused long enough for Nat to give an uncertain nod, surprised at the turn their conversation had taken.

"I want you to do something for the girl. I want you to transform her into the look of a boy. Cut her hair and dress her in your spares, at least until she can purchase some of her own."

"What?" Nat stared at the captain. "You can't mean what you said. She'll not stand for it. Why would you do such a thing?"

Captain Paderwatch gave a slight smile as though amused by his protest.

"She may not look it now," Nat persisted, "but you have only to talk with Miss Samantha to know she comes from a good family. She's been raised well. Why would you ask me to take away such a critical part of her being?"

Purchase a copy at your
local bookstore or preferred online vendor.

About the Author

 Margaret McGaffey Fisk is a story-teller who explores tales across gen-res and worlds. Raised in the Foreign Service where she developed a love for anthropology, she has been a data entry clerk, veterinary tech, editor, support engineer, and programmer, among other roles. She pulls on her studies and experiences to give depth to the cultures and people that form the heart of her stories. As her website is titled, she offers tales to tide you over.

She'd love to hear from you through any of the contact points or social media accounts listed on her website, or you can subscribe to one of her newsletters for release announce-ments, snippets, and other news: margaretmcgaffeyfisk.com/subscribe-to-my-newsletter/

Website
MargaretMcGaffeyFisk.com

Acknowledgements

I'd like to thank David Bridger for encouraging me to write this series after hearing the barest idea and making sure the story never fell off the table until he got the chance to read it.

My husband Colin deserves thanks as always for supporting my publishing by proofreading my novels and performing numerous other tasks. A good number of folks helped out with cover and back cover text feedback, while special thanks still goes to my little sister, Deirdre, who contributed her face to make Samantha come alive.

As you can see, though I'm taking this indie journey, I am not walking it alone. The last piece of my publishing process, and the last essential group, is you, my readers. Thank you for allowing me to bend your figurative ear and for welcoming my characters into your lives.

www.ingramcontent.com/pod-product-compliance
Lightning Source LLC
Chambersburg PA
CBHW030626120726
47904CB00006B/2054